CW01238659

NICOLA JANE
PIT

THE CHAOS DEMONS MC
BOOK 4

PIT
The Chaos Demons MC
By
Nicola Jane

Copyright © 2024 by Nicola Jane.
All rights are reserved.

This book is a work of fiction. The names, characters, places, and incidents are all products of the author's imagination and are not to be construed as real. Any similarities are entirely coincidental.
No part of this book may be used or reproduced in any manner without written permission from the author,
except in the case of brief quotations used in articles or reviews. For information, contact Nicola Jane.

Cover Designer: Wingfield Designs
Editor: Rebecca Vazquez, Dark Syde Books
Proofreader: Jackie Ziegler, Dark Syde Books
Formatting: V. R. Formatting

SPELLING NOTE

Please note, this author resides in the United Kingdom and is using British English. Therefore, some words may be viewed as incorrect or spelled incorrectly, however, they are not.

TRIGGER WARNING

This book contains triggers for violence, explicit scenes, and some dirty talking bikers.
If any of this offends you, put your concerns in writing to Axel and he'll get back to you . . . maybe.

PLAYLIST:
DON'T SPEAK – NO DOUBT

Prisoner – Raphael Lake ft. Daniel Murphy & Aaron Levy
Demons – Imagine Dragons
The Heart Wants What It Wants – Selena Gomez
Renegade – Aaryan Shah
when the party's over – Billie Eilish
Fighter – Christina Aguilera
Mean – Taylor Swift
Breathe Me – Sia
Hey Bully – Morgan Frazier
Fix You – Coldplay
If I Ain't Got You – Alicia Keys
We Belong Together – Mariah Carey
Hate That I Love You – Rihanna ft. Ne-Yo
Out of Reach – Gabrielle
SLOW DANCING IN THE DARK – Joji
If the World Was Ending – JP Saxe ft. Julia Michaels
Better Together – Jack Johnson
I'm Yours – Jason Mraz

At Last – Etta James
Come Back Home – Sofia Carson

CHAPTER 1

PIT

I flick my cigarette and watch the orange glow splinter into the darkness. Crushing it with my heavy boot, I release the smoke from my lungs. Pulling my mobile from my pocket, I accept the call from my President and press the handset to my ear. "Pres?"

"Pit, I got a lead," he says. "I'm sending the location through to the burner."

"Kay," I mutter, disconnecting before stuffing it back in my pocket. I get out the burner phone and switch it on.

The Chaos Demons have been moving drugs and weapons from warehouses across London and over to countries that pay a good price for them. But recently, we've had to stop moving everything because the boys in blue are watching us closely, which means we have a lot of units sitting full, and now, they're being hit. One by one, they've been targeted and emptied, and we're now at a four-container loss.

I stare out across the Thames. The dark, murky water

offers me comfort, and I briefly close my eyes until the vibration of the phone forces me back to reality.

The address is only a few minutes away, but I head back to the bike and throw my leg over. If I leave it here, it'll get towed—London is savage for parking.

Minutes later, I pull up outside a large factory. Shadow, my Sergeant at Arms, and Grizz, my VP, are already waiting as I dismount and head over to where they wait. "Axel didn't say I'd have company," I mutter, shaking hands with each of them.

"Is it a problem?" Grizz asks.

"No problem," I reply, looking at the large building. "Are we going in or standing about talking?"

Grizz rolls his eyes and pushes the gate. It creaks open, and we edge towards the door. "You got a weapon?" he asks, looking back at me briefly before trying the door and finding it locked.

"No," I say, raising my boot and kicking it right in the centre. It pops open and I head inside.

"Fuck," mutters Grizz. "You're a loose cannon."

I pull out my phone and flick on the torch, illuminating the entrance hall. There's no sign of anyone, so I move to the first room, and again, it's empty. We continue on, opening each door to what used to be offices and finding no one.

"Pres showed us the floor plans before we came out. There's a basement," says Shadow.

"What are we waiting for?" I ask, wondering why the fuck it wasn't mentioned before.

We find the stairs that lead down, and as we get to the bottom, there's a metal gate with the lock off, slightly ajar.

I listen for a second, making out the sound of humming. Pressing my finger to my lips, I indicate for the other two to stay quiet as I gently ease the gate open wider. We slip through, and I peer around the wall, spotting stacks of crates. I grin and look back at the VP, giving him a nod. *Jackpot.*

We move into the room, ducking behind the crates until a desk comes into view. Sitting behind it is a man I don't recognise, but I know instantly he isn't the mastermind behind it all because he's too laid back with his feet propped up on the desk, a casual T-shirt and jeans, and a pair of Crocs. *Fucking Crocs.* I shake my head and stand fully, moving towards him quickly. He doesn't have time to remove his feet before I have him by the throat and pinned back in the chair. He coughs violently as I restrict the airflow.

"You've got some explaining to do," I growl, releasing his throat. He inhales sharply, pulling his feet from the desk. "What the fuck have you got on your feet?" I ask.

"Fuck's sake," hisses Grizz. "Seriously, what's your problem with Crocs?"

"They're impractical for a start. If you're gonna sit down here and guard shit this important, have some good footwear so you can run away when we arrive."

Shadow begins lifting the lids on crates. "This is them," he confirms.

I punch the guy in the nose, busting it. He groans, cupping his face. "And because of your stupid footwear, you now have blood on your feet. It'll pool in those shitty shoes and you'll slip around. You'll never be able to run."

"Cut the crap," snaps Grizz. He leans on the desk,

fixing the guy with a glare. "Who the fuck do you work for?"

"I just get paid to sit here," he cries, pinching the bridge of his nose to try and stem the bleeding.

"By?" Grizz pushes.

"I dunno."

I crack him in the face again. "Lies."

"I don't know," he wails louder. I deliver a precise blow to his stomach, and he doubles over, coughing again.

Grabbing a handful of his unwashed hair, I tip his head back so we're eye-to-eye. "Two seconds and I break your hand."

"I swear," he yells.

I snap his fingers back, and he screams in pain. "Let's try again."

"A man . . . important looking . . . suit, tie, the lot."

"I ain't here for a damn fairy tale," I growl. "I want names."

"We don't get that information. We just call him 'boss'." I take his other hand, and he cries out before I've even done anything. "Okay," he yells. "Okay, I'll tell you. Alec Clay."

"It means nothing," says Grizz.

I snap the man's fingers back, and he sobs uncontrollably. "Fuck, man, I told you what I know."

"Why's he taking our shit?" I ask. "How did he know about it?"

"He had a tip-off from a copper. He's got a buyer coming later tonight. This shit's worth some money."

"And don't we know it. But it ain't his, it's ours, and we're taking it back."

"He'll kill me," he cries desperately.

"We're gonna do that anyway," I say, taking a letter opener from the desk and dragging it across his throat. He gurgles, his eyes searching my face in the slight hope I may find a smidgin of decency. I won't. I never understand why they always look so confused, like they didn't think hanging in bad circles would lead them to this moment.

I let his head fall back. His hands grip the oozing blood to no avail, and his eyes widen as he realises he's taking his final breath. I watch the life drain from his eyes, smiling as he gasps one last time.

TESSA

Oh fuck. Oh fuck. Oh fuck. I press myself into the dark corner of the room and try to control my breathing.

"Pres, we got it all back. Shadow's just counting the crates, but it looks like it's all here. We got the name . . . Alec Clay mean anything?" I peer over the stacked crates to where a man in a leather jacket is pacing while talking into a mobile phone.

Another guy in the same jacket is tacking the lids back on some of the crates. The third man is staring into the eyes of Jackson Taylor. The dead eyes. *Holy shit, he's dead.*

I feel panic rising again, and I squeeze my eyes closed to try to calm my racing mind. I picture my house, the one I grew up in by the coast. *He's dead.* I think about Trixy, the family cat we had. *He slit his throat.* I picture my beautiful mother, sitting on her bed, combing her gorgeous curly hair. *I just witnessed a murder.*

"Well, well, well . . ." My eyes shoot open and I gasp, but before I can scream, his hand covers my mouth. *The same hand he just used to kill Jackson.* He drags me from the corner and presses my back to his front, keeping my mouth covered as he walks me out into the open. The other two men stop what they're doing to stare at me. "We have a problem."

"Pres, I'll call you back," says the man on the phone, disconnecting the call. "Who the fuck are you?"

The man holding me uncovers my mouth, and I inhale sharply as he takes a handful of my hair instead. "You scream and I'll kill you," he warns.

"Te-Te-Tessa," I stutter.

"Well, Te-Te-Tessa, what are you doing here?" he demands.

My brain freezes. If I tell them I'm here because of Alec, they might kill me too. "Sex," I manage to say.

"You want sex?" asks the man, smirking.

"No, I'm here for sex. He . . ." I point a shaky finger in Jackson's direction and a sob escapes me. "He brought me here."

"Lies," states the man holding me. He tugs my hair harder, and I whimper. "Treat me like a personal lie detector," he hisses in my ear. "Now, get fucking talking before you end up like him." He forces my head to look in the direction of Jackson, and I close my eyes.

"I swear it," I say, my tone pleading. "It was just a hook-up."

The other man's phone rings again and he sighs. "It's the Pres again. I gotta tell him." He steps away.

The other guy checks his phone. "The van is here. I'll start loading."

"Just you and me now, Te-Te-Tessa," the man holding me hisses in my ear. I swallow the lump of anxiety in my throat. "How do you know him?"

"I don't," I say, shaking my head and causing his hold to pull tighter. I wince. "It was a hook-up app."

"Show me," he snaps, running his hand down my side until he finds my mobile in my back pocket. He holds it in front of me and the facial recognition opens it. *Fuck. Now what?*

"Look," I begin, holding up my hands in a placating manner, "I don't want to be here any more than you do. Just let me leave and we'll pretend we never met."

"Nice try," he mutters, scrolling through my apps, looking for one I know he won't find.

"I deleted the app," I lie.

He tugs my head back harder, and I cry out. "You better start talking, bitch, cos I'm losing my patience."

"Okay," I yell. "Okay."

The other man returns, tucking his mobile away. "We gotta take her," he says.

I shake my head. "No, please. I didn't see anything. I won't say anything to anyone. Please." I'm openly sobbing, but I don't care. I can't go with these men.

The man holding me keeps my phone and uses my hair to direct me from the basement. He doesn't seem to care I have nothing on my feet. *Why the fuck did I take my heels off?* Not that I could run in them anyway. *How the hell did my life turn to this?* I almost scoff at myself out loud. I know exactly how—Alec fucking Clay.

CHAPTER 2

PIT

I use tape to secure the woman's hands behind her back, then I crouch before her to do the same to her ankles. That's when I notice there are no shoes on her feet. I glance up in confusion, right as she kicks me in the balls. I groan, dropping to my knees, and she shoves me hard so I fall back. She's out the van and running before I can even call to Shadow, who's still loading crates in the back.

"Fuck," I mutter, jumping to my feet and running after her.

She's short, like five-foot-three at most, and her hands are taped behind her back, so it's seconds before I'm right behind her. She stumbles, falling to the ground and rolling a few times before coming to an abrupt stop. I grab a handful of her hair and pull her to her feet. She cries out, and I sense her frustration as I wrap my free hand around her neck. She gasps, and I press my forehead to hers. "You're more trouble than you're worth," I growl, squeezing harder.

Her eyes meet mine, the blue shining under the moonlight, and then she relaxes. It's an odd reaction to the pressure I'm placing on her throat while still holding her hair in my fist. Usually, they kick and flail about, but this bitch . . . she's looking me dead in the eye, as if daring me to end her life. Her small hand takes my wrist gently and then she closes her eyes.

"What the fuck?" I snap, shoving her back, and she stumbles, almost landing on her backside. She's freaking me out. "Don't run again or I'm gonna slit your throat, are we clear?" Without another word, she heads back to the van and slides into the backseat. I stare after her in confusion before catching Shadow's eye.

"You okay, brother?"

"The bitch just kicked me in the balls," I say, as if that explains it all, and then I head after her.

She's staring straight ahead. This time, when I slide my hand down her bare leg, she allows me to wrap the tape around her ankles. "Where are your shoes?" I ask.

"Fuck you."

I snigger. *That's more like it.* "Fine, stay barefoot." I slam the van door and lean against it, taking out a cigarette and lighting it while ignoring the throbbing ache in my balls.

Once the van is loaded, I head back inside and empty the contents of a petrol can around the body. I light it and leave, not bothering to look back. The fucker should never have crossed The Chaos Demons.

BACK AT THE CLUBHOUSE, Axel holds his head in his hands. "We need to find out who this Alec fucker is. And that bitch needs hiding until I decide what to do with her."

"She's given us nothing," says Grizz.

"She's a witness," states Axel. "We can't leave her to talk."

"But she's also a woman, someone's daughter," Coop points out.

"Don't give me that shit, Coop," snaps Axel. "What are we meant to do?"

"She's probably scared out of her wits, Pres," he argues. "She'll talk. Give her a chance to process."

"And then what?" I snap. "She processes, and we let her go off into the sunset?"

"Maybe," he says, shrugging.

"Bullshit," I snap. "She saw me kill a man. I ain't risking her getting out of here and talking."

"Then you should've checked the coast was clear," says Coop. "At least let me talk to her."

"And let her see another brother?" asks Axel. "No way."

"All I'm saying is, she might be innocent in all this. She's young. We might be able to scare her into keeping her mouth shut."

"No," snaps Axel. "She dies," he adds, making the final decision.

"Pres," Coop mutters, sighing, "we gotta vote on that shit."

"Not when it's for the good of the club. I can't put that decision on you guys," he says. "It's on my head."

"I think Coop's right," adds Fletch. "We should at least

find out her story. Coop is good at talking to women. Let him try."

Axel groans. "Fine, but she can't stay here. If Lexi or any of the women see her, they'll do that chick shit they do, and before we know it, she'll be part of the club." A few of the men snigger. "Pit, you got a place she can stay?"

"Are you serious?" I snap. "She witnessed me kill, and now, I've got to put her up like I'm an Airbnb?" It raises a few more sniggers.

"Well, Coop is right. You didn't check the warehouse, so this is partly your fault."

I roll my eyes and push to stand. "Great. And how long am I keeping her around?"

"I'll send Coop over tomorrow to chat with her. Keep her alive until then," Axel orders.

I pull the door open. "I ain't making no promises."

I go into Axel's office, where the girl is still sitting after I dumped her on the couch. Her eyes widen when I force her to stand. I had taped her mouth, even though she made no attempts to talk. I throw her back over my shoulder and head for the exit. As we pass a prospect, I nod for him to follow me out.

Dumping her back on her feet by my bike, I pull out a flick knife. She flinches, and I smirk before cutting away the tape from her ankles. "I'm gonna sit you on my bike," I tell her, tipping her chin back so we're making eye contact. "Then my prospect here is gonna tape your hands around me. You cause me any problems, I'll end you right here." She gives a nod.

I throw my leg over the bike then lift her and place her

on the front, facing me. I position her legs over my thighs, pulling her close enough that no one can see her underwear. I cut her hands free and force them around my waist, pressing her face to my chest, then Smoke proceeds to tape her hands behind me. With my kutte in place, no one can see that she's bound. The prospect hands me my spare helmet, and I push it on her head and slide the visor down. "I hope you like dogs," I mutter, starting the engine before pushing my own helmet on.

The ride to my place is less than ten minutes. I drive down into the basement parking and go to my allocated space. I remove my helmet, followed by hers, then lift her and stand, keeping her legs around me as I get off the bike. Lowering her feet to the floor, I shift her so she's tucked in my side. Now, it just looks like she's my loving woman, clinging to me. I throw my arm around her, and we head for the elevator.

"Keep your head down," I order as we step inside. There are cameras in here, and although I can wipe them once I get to my apartment and get the software up on my laptop, I don't want security seeing us and coming up to question me.

Before the doors slide open, I pull the tape from her mouth. She hisses. "You make a sound and it'll be your last."

The elevator stops at the floor before mine, and I growl in frustration. I move Tessa to the corner, and as two men step in, I tilt her head back so she's staring into my eyes. I brush my thumb over her cheek, and she inhales sharply as her pupils dilate and her tongue darts out to wet her lower lip. I smile, running my hand down her cheek and resting it against her throat. I gently press my lips to hers, and she opens wider, allowing me to sweep my tongue into her mouth. A small whimper escapes her, and I press harder against her throat, a silent warning not to speak up even though her whimper doesn't sound like she hates the kiss.

The door opens to my floor and I break the kiss, then I stride from the elevator with her pressed to my side.

Gigi and King sense my arrival and begin to bark from behind the apartment door. I feel her pull back slightly, and I glance down at her wide, frightened eyes. "Don't worry, they only kill on command," I say dryly, pushing my key into the lock and opening the door.

My two pit bulls rush out, wagging excitedly while circling us. "Enough," I say firmly, and they still. "Inside." They head in with us following.

"I don't like dogs," she whispers.

"I don't like lying bitches, so we have things in common."

I shrug from my kutte and place it on the hook. I pull out the pocketknife and feel to my side, slicing the tape from her wrists. She immediately steps back, putting space between us. "Through there," I order, giving her a small shove towards the living room. Gigi and King are sitting waiting in the middle of the room. Tessa stops in her tracks, and Gigi immediately stands with her ears pointed forward and her tail still. "She thinks you're going to attack," I tell Tessa casually. "Relax."

"Easy for you to say," she whisper-hisses. "She's not eyeing you up like you're her next meal."

"I told you, she won't kill unless I give the order."

Tessa keeps her eyes trained on me as I approach the

dogs and pat them. "Sit." When Tessa doesn't move, I look back at her. "I'm talking to you."

She carefully edges towards the couch, keeping her eyes fixed on the dogs. Gigi relaxes, sitting back down and looking to me for instruction. "Easy," I tell her gently, tickling her behind her ear. "Go lay by the door." They do as I say, leaving the room.

"There's one way out," I tell Tessa. "Two if you count the window," I add, pointing to the floor-to-ceiling glass, "but it's a long way down. And if you choose the door, make no mistake, the dogs will attack."

"Who are you?" she asks, her eyes darting around the room like she's looking for some kind of clue. She won't find it here. I hardly stay in this apartment. It's a place to rest my head when I need it, but I spend most of my time on the road, doing jobs for the club. Settling in one place just isn't for me.

"I'm the last man you'll ever see," I tell her. "By this time tomorrow, you'll no longer be my problem and I'll be back on the road."

"What does that mean?" she asks, her brows furrowing.

"That no matter what you say, I ain't letting you live."

Her eyes widen. "What?"

"You're a witness. I can't have you opening that pretty little mouth of yours."

"But I won't. I told you, I'll stay quiet."

I give a small laugh. "Well, excuse me if I don't believe you. Now, get some rest."

She stares at the couch. "Why are you waiting? If you're going to kill me, just get it over with."

I sit on the armchair opposite her. "I have to wait for the go-ahead."

"What if it doesn't come?"

I shrug. "I'll say you tried to run and the dogs got crazy. Putting you down was the kindest thing to do."

She frowns deeper. "You're a real piece of work," she mutters.

I grin proudly. "I know."

TESSA

I watch the man lean back in the chair. He's relaxed, like all this is normal, just like the way he speaks of death. *Normal.* I shiver involuntarily, unable to stop my mind racing. He cannot be the last man I see. He can't be the last man I kiss. *The kiss.* Fuck, I might be scared out my mind, but that kiss was good. *How fucked-up is that?*

He tugs his hood from his head, giving me the first good look at his face. There's a large scar running from his temple, across his cheek, and down his neck. It's hidden well along the line of his beard, disappearing under his neck tattoos, and I find myself wondering what kind of situation he got into that caused such a huge wound.

"People will be looking for me," I say.

He leans his head back on the chair and closes his eyes. "I don't care."

"My parents know I was at the warehouse."

"Good. They'll think you died in a fire."

I rub my sweaty hands over my dress, wishing I'd worn something more appropriate tonight. "They won't, not without a body. They're very persistent."

He sighs heavily and lifts his head to fix me with his dark eyes. "Tessa, isn't it?" His tone is bored. "I don't give a crap about your sob story. I'll dump your body on their front lawn and walk away in broad daylight."

"Don't you have an ounce of empathy?" I snap. "Don't you care I have a family?"

He rolls his eyes and pulls out my mobile. He leans forward to try and get my facial profile to open it again, but I turn away. "I haven't felt it vibrate," he says, standing. "No one's blowing it up asking where the hell you are." He pushes me back against the couch and grips my chin, pointing the phone at my face until it gives him access. He takes a seat beside me, and I shift away as much as possible. "See, no missed calls." He opens my messages, and I briefly close my eyes and curse in my head. "Well, what do we have here?" he asks, opening the top message. "Alec?"

"That's private," I snap, trying to grab the phone from him. It's a stupid move because, with little effort, he takes my throat and pins me back again while he continues to read out the messages.

"Alec, where the fuck are you? There's someone in the warehouse. Please come and get me." He turns his glare to me. "You better get talking, bitch."

I groan. "It's not what you think."

He throws my phone on the table and turns himself so he's facing me, still keeping me pinned back. "What I think is that you and this fucker are a thing."

"We're not."

"So, why are you asking him for help?"

"Because . . . because he left me there."

"Why?"

"He said it would be simple. Stay there until the delivery was done. Call him and he'd come and get me."

"Why would he leave you to oversee a million-pound deal?"

"I don't know."

"Oh, darling, if you knew how pissed I'm getting, you'd be singing like a fucking canary right now." He releases me and stands, getting his own mobile phone out. "Gigi," he calls, and the faithful mutt rushes in. "Watch," he tells her, pointing to me. She sits facing me, and I pull my legs up, tucking them under me and away from her sharp teeth. "You move and she'll rip your limbs off." And then he disappears into another room.

I stare at the dog, and she stares at me. I offer a weak smile, and she lifts her lip in a snarl. "You really love him," I mutter, and she snarls louder. "Go," I whisper, wondering if she listens to anyone else, but she remains seated. "Leave. Door. Go. *Fuck*." Her brown eyes don't leave me. "Jesus, this is like some film. A nightmare I can't wake from."

It's minutes before he returns, but it feels like hours with the dog staring at me with such hatred. "Relax," he tells her, and she trots off. *Relax. Why Didn't I think of that?* "Get some rest."

"You think I can rest after all this?" I spit angrily. "I just want to go home."

"My President wants to speak with you tomorrow."

"Why?"

"Cos he wants to know who the fuck is taking us on, and you have the answer to that."

I shake my head. "I don't. I absolutely do not know anything."

"Sleep, Tessa. Save your lies for tomorrow."

∼

I DON'T SLEEP. It's impossible with him sitting opposite me. He rests his eyes occasionally but spends most of the night watching me. And so, I toss and turn until the sun lights up the room.

The man stands and stretches before disappearing again. This time, when he returns, he's eating cereal from a bowl. My stomach growls in hunger, and he sniggers, heading towards the large window and staring out.

There's a knock at the door, and the dogs bark until the man orders them to shut up. He goes to answer the door, returning with two more well-built men, all wearing the same jackets. The second man sits down opposite me and smiles. He's older with kinder eyes, and he nods to the other two so they leave the room. "I'm Coop," he tells me.

"Tessa," I almost whisper.

"You had a drink and some food, Tessa?" he asks.

I shake my head, and he curses under his breath. "Hey, Pit," he calls, and my kidnapper returns. "Feed the girl," he snaps, "and get her a drink."

"It's not a hotel," he replies.

"Would it kill yah to at least get some water?"

My kidnapper rolls his eyes and disappears, returning in seconds with a bottle of water and a banana. I take it eagerly. I haven't eaten since yesterday morning. Coop waits while I eat and then he unscrews the cap on the water, handing it to me. "Small sips," he says, "or you'll throw it back up." I follow his instruction. "What were you doing at that warehouse last night?"

I take a breath, knowing my next words could either land me in deeper or set me free. I go with the truth. "Alec asked me to wait there while the deal went down."

"What deal?"

"For the crates. He went off to meet the guy and was bringing him back to the warehouse. He was only supposed to be half an hour, but I was waiting at least an hour."

"Did he say who he was meeting?" I shake my head. "Darlin', it'd be real helpful if you told me everything cos, otherwise, I don't get a choice in what happens next."

"Your man is going to kill me anyway. He said so."

"It's not up to him," he reassures me. "How do you know Alec?" I bite on my lower lip. "I need it all," he pushes.

"It was supposed to be a few days' work," I mutter. "I needed the cash."

"What do you do?"

"Escort," I admit, lowering my eyes to the ground.

"Don't be ashamed," he tells me gently. "You're just trying to survive out there like the rest of us."

"He said it would be for three days and he'd pay me after."

"First rule of business, darlin', always get payment up front. You been doing it for long?" he asks, and I shake my head. "Yeah, I can tell," he adds with a smirk. "So, where's this guy live?"

"I don't know."

"Come on," he says with a groan.

"I don't, honestly. We stayed in a hotel the first night, and that day, he was doing business dealings. We got to the warehouse, he got a call to meet someone, and the rest I told you."

"So, you've never met him before a few days ago?" I shake my head. "And he doesn't know anything about you?" I shake my head again. "Okay, let me see what I can do." He stands and goes to find the others.

CHAPTER 3

PIT

"What the fuck is wrong with you?" asks Coop, coming into the kitchen. "You don't feed her or give her a drink?"

"She's not a damn guest," I snap. "And when she dies, she won't shit herself if she's empty."

"Fuck, Pres, do something about him, would yah?"

Axel shakes his head in annoyance. "He's a lost cause. Did she talk?"

"Yeah."

I glare at Coop. "She did?" I can't hide the surprise in my tone.

"Yeah, amazing what some respect and kindness gets you," he says, arching a brow. "She's an escort. He hired her for a few days, they went to the warehouse last night, and he left her there while he went to a meeting. He didn't return."

"So, she doesn't know him?" asks Axel.

"No. Never met him before, and he didn't pay her either."

"I know what you're trying to do here," I snap, "and she ain't gonna live past today."

"She's done nothing wrong," Coop argues.

"She saw me," I yell.

"She won't talk."

"And if she does?"

"What will she tell them, that some guy with two dogs took her and held her for the night? She's an escort. She'll stay quiet cos the police won't give a shit. They'll think she pissed some customer off and she's trying to get paid or something."

"I ain't risking it," I tell them. "She dies today."

A phone rings, and I realise it's in my pocket. I take it out. "It's Tessa's," I tell them, glancing at the screen. "It's him," I add, showing them Alec's name.

Axel takes it and accepts the call, putting it on loudspeaker. "Tessa, where are you?" Alec yells, sounding panicked. "What the fuck happened? Who came to the warehouse and took my shit? Jackson is dead."

"I think you'll find it was my shit to begin with," Axel says calmly.

The line falls silent for a few seconds. "Who the hell is this?"

"The person you stole from," Axel replies.

"Impossible. Where the fuck is she? Where's Tessa?"

"She's safe, for now."

"Put her on," he demands.

"Yah know, Mr. Clay, you've really pissed me off," says Axel. "So, I think you should reel in the tantrum and stop making demands."

"You know my name," he states. "At least offer me the same courtesy and give me yours."

"Axel. I'm the President of The Chaos Demons."

The line falls silent again. "So, you found me," he says, sounding amused. "The problem is, Axel, those crates have already been sold, and if my buyer doesn't get them, he's going to come looking for you."

"I don't see why. They were never yours to sell, therefore, I'm not the one who can't deliver."

"You have no idea who you're messing with."

"I think you're the one who's confused," says Axel.

"You'd better return those crates and my fucking wife," he screams before disconnecting.

I arch a brow. "Wife?" I repeat, staring at Coop in amusement. Seems he didn't get the entire truth after all.

I storm into the living room where Tessa is staring out the window. She turns just as I shove her against the glass. I pin her arms above her head and press my mouth to her ear. "You're his wife," I growl. "His fucking wife."

"It's not what you think," she cries, twisting to try and get free.

"I was trying to help you," says Coop from behind me, his voice laced with disappointment. "All you had to do was tell the truth."

She laughs . . . actually laughs. "And then you'd have let me go, right?" She huffs in annoyance. "He'll come for me," she spits. "I bet he's already on his way."

"Tracker," mutters Axel, "in her phone."

"He'd have used that to find her last night," I snap. "She's talking shit."

She looks me in the eye and grins. "Wanna wait around to find out?"

I reach into my boot and retrieve a small knife. "You're right, let's put an end to it." I press the blade to her neck, and she freezes, her confidence from seconds ago vanishing.

"Pit," snaps Axel, "stop."

"Why? Let's just end her now and concentrate on the real problem."

"We can use her," he says. "Let her go."

I keep my eyes trained on her baby blues. They dilate, and then she turns her head slightly, breaking eye contact. I step back, and she releases a breath, rubbing her wrists. "We need to move her," adds Coop.

"I got another place," I mutter.

"I'll keep her phone and get one of the guys to check for any trackers just to make sure. I need to keep contact with this fucking idiot," Axel says. "In the meantime, get her talking."

∼

I DRIVE HALF an hour to the farm I inherited from my grandparents over ten years ago. Gigi and King immediately begin barking, recognising where we are. The noise wakes Tessa, and she looks out the window at the rundown farmhouse. "Where are we?"

I smirk, getting out the truck and slamming my door. I let the dogs out before rounding her side and opening the door. I lift her and carry her towards the house, seeing as her wrists and ankles are bound again.

I dump her on the large wooden kitchen table, resting her feet on the bench, then I go to the drawer, retrieve a large knife, and cut the tape from her ankles. She holds out her arms expectedly, and I shake my head. "No, just the ankles."

"You can't keep me like this," she argues. "What if I have to pee?"

"Do you?"

"Maybe," she mutters.

"Follow me," I tell her as I head for the back door. She struggles down from the table and follows me into the overgrown garden. I lead her down the garden path to a small shed that houses the outside toilet. I pull the dilapidated door and it creaks open.

I point, and she peers inside. "This is the toilet?"

"Do you still need to pee?" She gives her head a slight shake. "I didn't think so." I head back inside, and she follows. "We're miles from anywhere," I tell her. "And the dogs run fast. You try anything and they'll hunt you down."

"How long are you keeping me here?"

"Until I'm told otherwise."

"I can't give you any information," she says, moving closer to me as Gigi comes into the kitchen. Tessa throws herself at me, keeping her eyes fixed on the dog. "Please, can't you keep that thing outside?"

"She's practically my child," I scoff, taking her by the arms and moving her a few steps back from me. "Feel free to go out there yourself, though."

"You'd make me live out there over a bloody dog?" she demands.

"Yep."

She narrows her eyes. "Now, what?" she asks, looking around.

"Now, we wait."

"For?"

"Your man to come to your rescue."

"Then what?"

"He'll die. And you . . . well, let's hope there's a plot for the two of you so you can be buried together."

TESSA

We've been here for hours and the sun is starting to set, so it must be at least nine in the evening. I don't know if Alec will get me out of this mess, but something tells me he won't, and then I'll be left to die at the hands of this fucked-up piece of shit who keeps scowling at me and refuses to engage in any kind of conversation.

I sit at the kitchen table with my hands resting on top, still taped together. I'm desperate for a pee, but there's no way I can go outside. There were spiders as big as the damn dogs in that thing.

Pit chops vegetables, and if it wasn't such a serious situation, I'd laugh. This huge, burly man chops the carrots with ease, occasionally emptying the pile into a pan. The potatoes are already on the boil, all things he got from the garden, like he's some kind of gardening wizard.

"So, have you had this place long?" I ask. So far, he's ignored my questions, only answering when he has some threat or a sarcastic comment to make.

He sighs before asking, "How long have you been married?"

I twist my fingers together. "Not long."

"A week, a month, a year?"

"A few days."

He frowns. "And you're already in the shit. Not really the marriage you'd hoped for? Was it a big affair?"

"Huh?"

"Your wedding, cos I checked your phone earlier and there were no pictures."

"So what?"

"Not really the sort of thing you'd expect from a blushing bride. I mean, how old are you and you haven't even got social media?"

"I don't like social media."

"Bullshit. People who don't have social media are hiding something."

"Do you have it?" I ask.

"No, but I'm hiding something."

"The fact you're a cold-blooded killer?"

He smirks, turning to put the pan of vegetables on the cooker. He grabs the pack of meat he took out the freezer earlier and slaps it on the chopping board, using a knife to cut away the packaging. "Where are you from, Tessa?"

"Why do you care if you're going to kill me?" I snap.

"My grandparents left me this farm," he says, placing two steaks on the board. I watch as he seasons them, occasionally rubbing the herbs into the red meat. The blood on his fingers takes me back to the warehouse, and I squeeze my eyes shut to block it out. "They died."

"Died, or did you kill them for it?" I ask, unable to stop myself.

He sniggers, and I'm relieved he hasn't taken offence. "They died together but not at my hands."

I roll my eyes, not believing him. "I wasn't lying. I don't know Alec," I tell him.

His eyes meet mine, and I stare back so he can see I'm telling the truth. "You married a man you don't know?"

"Yes."

"Why?"

"That's none of your business. I have my reasons, but I didn't lie about anything else."

"So, you are an escort?"

"Of sorts."

"He hired you to marry him?"

"I have something he wants."

"Well, now, I have something he wants too, so let's hope he's willing to fight to get it all back."

He turns his back and places the steaks in a red-hot pan. As they sizzle, I stand, gaining the attention of Gigi, who also stands, alerting Pit, who turns. "I'm not running," I snap. "I need to pee."

"So, pee," he says, nodding at the door.

"With my hands tied?" I ask.

"Yes."

"In that spider-filled shack outside?"

"Yes."

"Fuck," I hiss, heading for the door. I step outside and look around. There's land for miles, and all I can hear are birds singing their evening song and crickets in the grass. I carefully open the door to the toilet and wince. There are cobwebs and huge spiders in the corners. I edge in slowly and look into the toilet. It's dirty inside, but there are no insects, so I squeeze my eyes closed and reach under my dress to remove my underwear. *If I can't see them, they're not there, right?* Lowering onto the seat, I breathe in through my nose and out through my mouth. "It's fine," I whisper out loud. "I'm fine. They're just little, tiny insects. They're scared of me and I'm bigger."

"Who are you talking to?" My eyes shoot open to find Pit staring at me with a confused look on his face.

"Myself," I hiss.

"You're giving yourself a pep talk about spiders?"

"I hate them," I admit.

"Pity, there's one right next to you," he says, and I scream, jumping off the toilet and running out with my underwear still around my knees. I'm aware I'm still screaming and waving my arms around my head, and it's only when Gigi runs at me that I fall back onto my arse.

"Gigi, sit," Pit orders when she's inches from my face. He's still half-laughing from my overreaction. "She's already terrified enough without you trying to eat her."

My heart slams against my chest, and I begin to sob. The last twenty-four hours are catching up with me, and being so terrified has come to a head. Pit's laughing fades. "Look," he says with a sigh, "I was kidding. It wasn't that big." I sob harder, trying to tug my knickers up my legs to no avail.

Pit swoops down and lifts me under my arms, putting me back on my feet. He crouches before me and pulls my knickers up, straightening my dress. "You're fine," he says firmly. "Spiders won't hurt you."

I give a slight nod, humiliation now replacing my terror. As I follow him back to the house, he begins to laugh again. "You know what's funny?" he asks, wiping tears from under his eyes. "That you reacted more to a fucking spider than you did to being taken or a man being killed right before your eyes."

We go back into the kitchen and the steaks are now resting in the pan. I'm impressed with his cooking skills—I've never known a man to cook before. My father was a lazy fuck who made me do everything he classed as 'woman's work', and I haven't known Alec long enough, but he seems the type to have a chef or just eat out a lot.

"Sit," he tells me, and I do.

He plates up the food, placing one in front of me, then he takes my wrists and uses a knife to slice the tape away. I rub the redness, grateful he's at least allowing me to eat properly.

He sits opposite me with his own plate of food and gives a nod. "I want to see what you think," he says.

I pick up the cutlery and slice into the steak. My mouth waters as the juices run out onto the plate. It's medium rare, cooked to perfection. I close my eyes in appreciation as it melts in my mouth, and when I open my eyes, Pit is watching me closely. "It's really good," I tell him, blushing slightly.

"We have cows," he tells me. "I have a farm manager who deals with all that, but there's enough meat in that freezer to feed half of London."

"Why don't you look after them?"

He shakes his head, taking a bite of his steak and groaning in pleasure. I shudder at the sound, picturing the way he kissed me in the elevator. "I don't stick around for long."

"Why?"

"So, what do you have that your husband wants?" he asks, changing the subject.

"That's my secret to keep."

He smirks. "It must be important if he married you."

"It's worth a lot," I reply.

"You know I'm going to find out, right?"

I continue to eat. Who knows what he'll do when he finds out? And without it, I have nothing left to bargain with.

"Are you married?" I ask.

He laughs. "Fuck no."

"I didn't think so."

He narrows his eyes. "And why's that?"

"Men like you don't usually have a wife."

"And now you're analysing me?" he scoffs. "Tell me, pretty lady, what do you think you know about me?"

I shrug. "You said you're away a lot. Women don't usually put up with that unless they travel too, and I don't see anyone with you. You love your dogs more than kids, so you don't have your own kids."

"I could have them. Maybe they don't live with me."

I shake my head. "You have no compassion or empathy. Parents usually have that. You seem like a solitary kind of guy who hates being around people, and you have no tolerance for women."

"I have no problem with women," he snaps. "It's just ones who lie that piss me off."

"I think you have a bad relationship with your mum,

and your dad ran out when you were small or before you were born."

He scowls again. "You seem like the type to fuck around," he says. "Maybe play a few guys against one another. I bet you left school with one thing in mind, to find a rich man and have kids."

"You're way off the mark," I mutter.

"Bet you were popular at school, top bitch badge for you. Bet all the boys flocked, and you loved the attention," he continues. "A prick tease."

"I bet you didn't even attend school," I counter. "You were the sort to skip school and hang out with drug dealers and criminals."

"Now, that part you got right," he says, winking. "I made pretty girls like you wet with one look, and then I'd break their little, desperate hearts."

I roll my eyes. "You're so full of yourself."

We eat the rest of dinner in silence. Once we're done, I stand, and he follows me with his eyes as I take my plate to the sink. I begin to fill it with hot water and washing-up liquid, then I turn and take his plate, relieved to be doing something normal amongst all this chaos.

Once I've washed up, he stands. "I'll show you where you're sleeping."

I almost smile. This farmhouse is beautiful, if not a little neglected. I imagine the bedrooms to be cosy, and I'm so tired, I'm certain I'll be asleep the second my head hits the pillow.

He leads me up a flight of stairs, but we pass all the doors and go to the end of the hallway. He stands to one side of a second set of stairs. "Up there," he says. My heart begins to race again because I've already guessed that beyond that door at the top of the stairs isn't a cosy bedroom.

Climbing the steps warily, I push the creaky door. The smell of dampness is strong, and the only light is a faint glow of orange from the sunset. It illuminates piles of boxes covered in dusty sheets. "The attic?" I ask, looking back at him.

He remains on the bottom step. "Goodnight, Tessa."

"Are you shitting me?" I snap, tiredness getting the better of me. "You want me to sleep up here in this dirty attic?"

"Like I said before, this isn't a hotel stay." His stupid dogs come rushing up when he whistles. "Watch," he tells them, and they sit at the foot of the steps.

"Wait," I say as he turns to leave. "What if I need to pee again?"

"You'll have to call for me."

I purposely didn't drink anything at dinner to avoid filling my bladder, but still, I don't want to risk being up here and forgotten about. "Well, where will you sleep?" I ask.

He grins. "In my bedroom."

"Well, can't I . . . erm . . . can't I sleep in there on the floor?"

He laughs. "No."

"Please, Pit. I won't talk. I just don't like . . ." I glance back. "The dark."

"Goodnight, Tessa," he says, more impatiently this time. He leaves, and I stare at the dogs watching after him.

"Fuck."

I step into the room and look around. There's no bed, and I daren't touch anything in case I disturb spiders, or worse, rats. Shuddering, I head to the round window and wipe my hand over the dusty glass, clearing it enough for me to look outside. There are fields upon fields and no sign of life beyond this farm. Pulling a stool to the window, I sit down and notice a figure in the garden below. *Pit.* He begins to move, taking the stance of a martial arts fighter as he slices the air with his arms. Of course, he's into that sort of thing, he's fit with a body ripped as fuck. I groan. Trust me to be lusting after the psycho who's keeping me captive.

CHAPTER 4

PIT

"I got nothing," says Axel when I call him. "We're trying to find out who this fucker is and we're just coming up against brick walls. No one's heard of him, and I can't find one fucker who will admit to trading with him."

"So, what do we do?"

"I tried calling him back, but he's not picking up. Did you get anything from her?"

"Not really. She said they got married a few days ago but she doesn't know him."

"Do you believe her?" he asks.

"Yeah. She doesn't know him. She said she's got something he wants."

"What?"

"She wouldn't tell me."

"And you didn't force it out of her?" he asks, sounding surprised.

"I can if you want me to."

"Yeah. Fuck it, we've got nothing else."

"Okay. Let me try something and I'll get back to you."

It's the early hours of the morning, and as I creep up to the attic, I pray she's asleep. She looked exhausted, and a woman with no sleep becomes a problem. I find her curled up on a pile of boxes, sound asleep. Watching her closely, I take in her beauty. It's a shame I'm about to ruin it.

I unscrew the lid from the jar and empty the large spider into my palm. I take it by the leg and dangle it over her face, gently brushing it over her lips. She swipes her hand across her face, and I wait for her to settle before doing the same thing again. This time, her eyes shoot open, and before she can react, I wrap a hand around her throat. Something about my tattooed hand splayed across her throat turns me the fuck on. I snigger as her eyes focus on the spider as it wriggles its legs, trying to grip onto something. Her eyes widen, but she daren't open her mouth because it's too close to her lips. "I wanna know what you have that your thieving husband wants."

She gives her head a slight shake, her eyes still wide with fear. I place the spider on her cheek, slapping her hand down when she tries swipe it off. She silently sobs, frozen in fear. "Tessa, it's simple, tell me what I want to know or I'll keep them coming." She remains silent as tears leak from each corner of her eyes.

I take the spider from her cheek and throw it to the floor. She releases a long, unsteady breath, and then her anger sets in. She begins to flail around, her legs and free arm coming at me. Her elbow catches my eye, and I hiss. "You fucking arsehole," she screams while I try to get her under control. "Who does that?"

"Jesus," I snap, finally getting hold of her wrists. I push them to her chest and lean my weight on her. Her legs still, but she pants heavily. "Tell me what I want to know," I demand.

"Fuck you," she spits.

"Suit yourself," I hiss, hauling her up and throwing her over my shoulder.

"Pit," she yells, whacking her fists against my back, "put me down."

I head downstairs and straight out into the garden. It isn't until I get closer to the toilet shed that she begins to panic, screaming and fighting against me. I throw her into the shed, pulling the door closed and holding it. "Pit," she screams in terror. "Please. Let me out." She bangs the door hard, shaking it with each thump. "Please," she begs. "I'm sorry. Please. I'm sorry. Let me out, please. Please." And then the banging stops and all I can hear is sobbing. I feel a sharp stab in my chest. It's a feeling I don't often get, and I shut it down. I don't have time for guilt.

I pull the door open, and Tessa falls out in a heap on the ground. She scrambles quickly along the concrete, not bothering that her legs are bare. She stops at my feet and collapses into a sobbing mess. "I'm a virgin," she cries into her hands. "He paid for my virginity."

I inhale sharply. They're not the words I expected to hear from her. I push down the urge to pick her up from the floor, instead leaving her there as I head back inside. Pulling out my mobile, I call Axel. He answers on the second ring. "He's paid for her virginity," I tell him.

"What the fuck?"

"I haven't got all the details yet, but it's nothing important to us."

"We could use it," he says. "I'll call church and update the brothers. Keep her talking."

I disconnect and look out the kitchen window, surprised when I see King sitting beside Tessa, whimpering like a little bitch. I watch in amazement as he tentatively licks her hand. She stops sobbing and lifts her head to stare at the beast. Carefully, she pushes to sit up, and King moves so close, she has no choice but to allow him as he lays his head on her shoulder. She eventually wraps her arm around his neck and cries into his fur.

"Fuck me," I mutter, shaking my head.

I step out. "King," I bark. He doesn't move, and I arch a brow. "King," I repeat. "Heel." He reluctantly pulls away from Tessa and heads my way. "Don't look at me like that, you traitor," I whisper-hiss as he sits at my feet. "Wait until I tell Gigi what you did."

Tessa brushes her hand over her grazed legs. "Come inside," I tell her.

She carefully stands, wiping her hands over her wet cheeks. "I need a shower," she almost whispers.

"You can have one later," I say firmly, going up the stairs. She follows.

"I'm wet," she mutters.

"Wet?" I repeat in irritation. I get to the top of the stairs and turn to watch her. Her cheeks are red with what looks like embarrassment, and she keeps her eyes to the ground. "Why are you wet?"

She comes to a stop before me. "I was scared," she utters.

Realisation hits me that she's pissed herself in terror, and I wince, ignoring the guilt. "Right." I lead the way to the bathroom, pushing the door open. She goes inside and stares at the toilet in disbelief. "I'll get you a towel," I say, leaving her in there.

I get the towels from my bag because they're freshly washed and the ones here aren't. When I head back to the bathroom, I hear the shower running, so I step inside, gasping at the sight of Tessa standing naked in the centre of the bathroom. She immediately tries to cover up, but it's too late. I've committed her to memory and my cock is already straining. I hold out the towel, and she takes it, holding it in front of her. I'm tempted to be a bigger dick and stay, but I've already pushed her over the edge, so I back out and close the door.

TESSA

Sickness fills my stomach as the adrenaline begins to leave my system. I begin to shake uncontrollably as I step from under the water and wrap myself in the soft, fluffy towel. I have no control as more tears slip down my cheeks. Now I've started, I can't seem to stop. I stare at my wet dress and underwear, realising I can't put those back on, and as if Pit's read my mind, he taps on the door before pushing a handful of clothes into the room. I take them gratefully. "I don't know if any of it will fit," he says through the door, "but it's the smallest I have."

I unravel the two shirts, taking the smallest and slipping my arms through, then I tie it at the waist. I hold up a pair of gym shorts and a pair of soft cotton bottoms.

Deciding to go with the bottoms, I slide them on. They're too big, so I fold them over a few times to tighten them.

I step out to find Pit waiting. His two dogs are at his side, and the nicer one, King, wags when he sees me. Pit narrows his eyes in annoyance, and I almost smile. "You can sleep in there," he says, nodding to an open door. I head that way, keeping my wet clothes in my hand.

The bedroom is cosy and exactly how I'd imagined it to look with a thick, four-post wooden bed frame and a large mattress with fluffy blankets. The pillows are stacked high, and I imagine they're like sleeping on clouds. "Let me take those," he says, grabbing my wet clothes.

I hold on to them. "No, it's fine."

"Tessa, they'll stink your room out. Let me take them." He manages to remove them from me. "Sleep now. I'll see you in the morning."

Before he leaves, he turns back. "I got you a lamp," he mutters, looking at the soft glow from the bedside cabinet. "You said you didn't like the dark." And then he leaves, closing the door. I smile even though I try to fight it.

Sliding under the fluffy quilt, I groan with appreciation. It's minutes before my eyes get heavy and drift closed. All that excitement has done me in.

~

I WAKE to the smell of bacon. Noting my bedroom door is open, I carefully get out of bed and head towards it, looking out into the hall to see if the beasts are guarding me. When I see the hall is empty, I sigh in relief and make my way to the bathroom, where I use the toilet. *Fucking prick*. I can't believe he had me using that insect-infested shack yesterday. I shudder at the memory.

I make my way downstairs, where Pit is sitting at the table, tucking into a sandwich. He looks up, regarding me for a few seconds before turning his eyes back to the open laptop in front of him.

"Are you any closer to working out what Alec wanted with your crates?" I ask, taking a seat opposite him.

"There's bread in the cupboard and bacon in the fridge," he mutters without looking away from the laptop.

"How long are you keeping me here?" I ask, getting back to my feet and heading over to the fridge. "Where did you get bread and bacon from?" I add as an afterthought.

"Pigs," he mutters. "This is a farm, remember."

I shrug. "And the bread?"

He sighs heavily and turns to me. "I feel like I have a fucking wife all of a sudden. Eat the bacon, slice the bread, and shut the fuck up."

I roll my eyes and grab the bacon. "What about coffee?" I ask.

"Fuck's sake," he mutters in irritation. "It's in the cupboard, but only if you like it black cos we're fresh out of milk."

"I can only drink it with milk," I say.

He scoffs. "Well, sorry, princess, I didn't expect visitors, so I didn't get any in."

"Is there a shop around here?" I ask, hoping to God he tells me there's a town or something close by. At least then, if I get a chance, I can make a run for it in the hope I'll eventually find someone.

He fixes me with a glare, arching a brow, and I

swallow the panic in my throat. I'm pushing him to the limit. "You realise you're here as a prisoner, right? This ain't some holiday."

I give a stiff nod. "Good job really. I'd definitely rate you as poor for the toilet situation." My attempt to lighten the mood works, and he almost smiles before turning back to the laptop.

I make a sandwich and take a seat opposite him again. He slams the laptop closed and his troubled stare fixes on the table like that has some answers. After a few minutes of silence, I sigh, getting his attention. He waits for me to speak, so I force a weak smile. "I was just wondering what happens next."

"That depends on your husband."

I shudder at the term. Fuck. *Husband.* The second we signed the register, the realisation of what I'd actually agreed to weighed me down. The fact we never consummated because of Alec's deal might have been a sign. He was due to whisk me off to Dubai for our honeymoon the second the deal went through.

"What does that mean exactly?"

"How confident are you that he'll come to your rescue?" he asks, smirking.

Not at all, I think to myself, but I nod. "Very."

"Good, because you've bought yourself some extra time."

"I'm the bait?" I ask, and he grins. "You want him to come for me so you can get to him?"

"Yep, unless we find him before then."

"And if that happens?"

He stands, leaning across the table until his face is inches from mine. "Then we won't need you anymore."

"Either way, I don't get out of this?" My heart slams hard in my chest.

"Bingo, sweetheart."

∼

THE DAY DRAGS. Pit spends most of it away from me as his faithful mutts follow my every move, making the chance of escape impossible. I've checked the kitchen from top to bottom for weapons, but the cutlery is all gone, hidden out of sight.

It's late afternoon when the rumble of bikes fills the air. I rush to the window as a group of men dismount their bikes, all shaking hands with Pit. They carry boxes of beer around the side of the house, disappearing from view.

I sigh heavily and drop down onto the couch. There isn't even a damn television in this dump. King rests his head on my lap, and I smile. I've hated dogs since I was a kid, but this one is kind of cute and has taken a shine to me. I pat the space beside me, and he jumps up, curling himself around my legs. Gigi remains glaring at me, and I smirk. "Don't be jealous," I whisper. "He likes me."

"One word and she'll take your face off." I start at the sound of Pit as he saunters in with a beer in his hand. "Go to bed," he tells me.

I frown. "No."

"It wasn't a fucking request."

"It's early."

"Do we need to visit the shed outside?" he threatens.

I narrow my eyes but push to my feet. "Are you having a party?"

"I'm discussing plans on how to get rid of your body," he retorts.

I smirk, heading for the stairs. "May I suggest cremation? I don't want to lie underground with the insects." It's not a joking matter, but for some reason, I don't think he's going to kill me anytime soon, and until that day comes, I'm just going to have to charm him.

~

DARKNESS HAS FALLEN as music blares from outside. I place down the book I'd found in my bedside drawer and head over to the French doors. It's hard to see what's going on, so I carefully turn the key to unlock and push them open. The loud voices fill my room as I take a step onto the small balcony. In one corner is a metal, rusted table with a chair. I lower onto it and close my eyes, absorbing the sound of fun and laughter. It's been far too long since I last heard it. Smiling, I think back to my mum and how happy she always was. *Was.* I sigh, opening my eyes and peering over the edge of the balcony.

There's a fire burning in the centre of the men, and I notice a few women have joined them. Pit is the only one seated alone. Movement near the barn a few metres away catches my eye. A man is kissing a woman against the door. His hands wander her curves greedily, and I feel an ache in my chest. I've never had that kind of encounter, hence the V-card fully intact. It's not like I haven't dreamt of meeting a gorgeous man and having him ravish me like I'm his last meal. I've read every spicy romance book out there, but those men don't exist—not in my world, anyway.

I watch the way he holds her neck loosely but commanding. It's hot. His other hand is now in her shorts, moving fast while she grips onto his shoulders with her head thrown back in the throes of ecstasy. *Lucky bitch.*

He suddenly stops and turns his head to the group. "Hey, Pit, you joining us?"

My eyes widen. Two hot men? *Fuck.* That had never really crossed my mind. Pit shakes his head, and the other guy shrugs before grabbing the woman's hand and leading her into the barn and out of view.

I chew on my lower lip, leaning back in my chair and putting my feet up on the balcony rail. There's no denying Pit is hot as fuck. Even the scar running down his face adds something to his appeal. Dangerous—maybe that's it —but lord knows he's not the kind of man you'd want to get involved with. I mean, he murdered someone with just the flick of his wrist. And he's holding my life in his hands. If only he knew how worthless that was, he wouldn't bother.

I close my eyes and pictures of Pit enter my head. Is it wrong to fantasise about the man who's taken me and is threatening to end my life? Probably, but he's the closest I've been to hotness in my life, and somehow, I can't seem to push away thoughts of that kiss in the elevator. I smirk to myself and trail my hand down my stomach and into my trousers. I brush my fingers over my clit and shiver. I'm not innocent—I've seen porn and spent lots of time getting to know my own body.

My body relaxes as I work my fingers through my wet folds, sighing in content and forgetting the situation I'm currently in. I feel the warmth of an orgasm building and rub faster. My entire body stiffens as the delicious feeling takes control and I ride the waves of my orgasm. I allow my head to fall back while my body basks in the afterglow. Reality can wait a minute.

I eventually sit up and freeze. Pit's eyes are on me. There's no mistaking it as a smirk pulls up the corner of his mouth, letting me know he saw me. *Fuck.* My cheeks burn with embarrassment, and I push to my feet and rush back into my bedroom, slamming the door. Mortification chases away the elation I felt minutes ago. I pace a few times, taking deep, calming breaths. He saw me touch myself. *So what?* It's not like I was naked or anything. I nod to myself like that somehow makes it all better, then I pull open the bedroom door to go to the bathroom. The trusty mutts are at the end of the hall, and they both sit to attention, watching me as I edge slowly towards them.

The bathroom door swings open and a female practically falls out, slamming her hands against the wall to catch herself. She giggles and then realises I'm there and jumps back in fright. "Oh shit, sorry, I didn't know you were waiting."

"It's fine," I mutter, lowering my head.

"Who are you?" she asks.

"Nobody important."

She frowns. "Seriously, who are you? Were you downstairs cos I didn't see you?"

"No, I . . ." I glance back at my room. I don't know if I'm supposed to tell anyone why I'm here. It's not like she'll help me anyway, she's clearly friends with Pit. "I'm staying for a while." I wince, knowing those words will only lead to more questions.

"Pit never mentioned it." I glance up, and her eyes are narrowed suspiciously. "Does he know you're up here?" Before I can reply, she grabs my upper arm. King jumps into action, immediately barking at her. "Shut the fuck up, you stupid mutt," she hisses.

"What the fuck's going on?" It's Pit, and I almost cry in relief when he appears at the top of the stairs. "King, heel," he growls, and the dog stops fussing and goes to him. "Ebony, get the fuck off her," he orders, and the woman lets me go. I rub my arm and lower my head again.

"I thought she'd snuck in here," says Ebony.

"You reckon anyone would get past Gigi and King?" he asks, and I hear amusement in his voice.

"Then who is she?"

"None of your fucking business is who," he snaps. "Get back downstairs." She huffs and shoulder barges me as she leaves.

I continue to the bathroom, but before I can close the door, Pit snatches my wrist in his hand. I automatically flinch and stare at him in horror. His frown softens, and he gently pulls my hand towards his face, inhaling. I'm confused for a second until he smirks and slides my pointy finger into his mouth. His tongue swirls around it, and I stop breathing, staring in wonderment as he adds my middle finger. A low hum escapes from somewhere in the back of his throat, and the vibrations tickle my fingers. He drags the wet digits slowly, releasing them with a popping sound. I gasp, and he hauls me to him so that I fall against his chest. "Taste yourself on my tongue," he whispers, and before my brain can process, he tips my head back a fraction and seals his lips to mine, sweeping his tongue into my mouth. He pulls back and says, "Perfection."

CHAPTER 5

PIT

What the fuck was that? I turn and head downstairs before she can entrance me with those fucking sad eyes. Ebony is waiting for me by the back door. "Who is she?"

I frown. "I told you, none of your goddamn business."

"But you've always come back to me," she says, pouting.

"Darlin', a few times every six months or so does not mean you own me. You're just a club whore," I snap, and she flinches at my words. I blame Grizz for this bullshit. Since he made Luna, an ex-club whore, his old lady, he's given them all false hope.

"Did you meet her on your travels? Is this why you haven't been to see me this time?"

I groan, scrubbing my hands over my face. "You and me ain't happening again, Eb. Go find some other mug."

She tries to make a grab for me, and I step back. "I'm sorry," she cries. "You're right, I shouldn't overstep. I didn't mean to."

I shake my head in annoyance and go around her, heading back out to my brothers. The last thing I need is a club whore catching feelings. I grab a can of beer and take my seat back by the fire.

Grizz sits beside me. "He's looking for her," he mutters, keeping his voice low to avoid any of the women overhearing. "We're gonna try to make contact again tomorrow and ask for a meet."

"He's not gonna meet," I say.

"Depends how desperate he is to get her virginity. Is she talking more?"

I shake my head. "We got the guns back, Grizz. Can't we just put her in the ground and move on?"

He smirks. "You getting itchy feet staying around?"

"Something like that," I mutter.

"The Pres wants to find out what we can take from this fucker in exchange."

"We're seriously thinking of handing her back?"

"Brother, she's worth something to him."

"Who the fuck even does that?" I mutter, taking another drink and allowing a quick glance up to her room. The lights are out, and I relax slightly knowing there's no chance I'll bump into her again, cos quite honestly, I'm not sure how much control I have since knowing her little secret.

"It's a thing," says Grizz, nodding. "I've seen women online doing it. Damn internet makes everything so fucking easy these days."

"Why'd she marry him though?" I wonder out loud.

"Fuck knows. You're stuck here with her, so find out."

I shake my head. "The less we talk, the better."

I feel him staring at me, but I keep my eyes to the fire, scared there's something there he may recognise other than hatred. "You just keep her locked away?" he asks casually.

"Yeah, what else am I meant to do with her?"

He smirks. "I dunno. Pretty woman, single biker . . ." He laughs, and I narrow my eyes.

"Yah know, because of your love story, I've got fucking Ebony on my back. All the damn whores want their own happily ever after."

He scoffs. "Anything is possible."

"Fuck that," I say. "I ain't settling down, least of all with a whore."

"I said the same thing, brother. Sometimes it just creeps up on you and you lose control. Is that why you don't wanna talk to her?"

"No," I snap, finishing my beer and standing. "I'm hitting the sack. Sort yourselves out."

∼

I TOSS AND TURN, unable to sleep because my damn head is full of her. I eventually throw the covers back in irritation and head for the bathroom just as Tessa comes out. She spins to face me with just a T-shirt on that barely covers her backside. I narrow my eyes and ask, "Is that my shirt?"

She glances down, gripping the hem and tugging it down some. "I borrowed it. I had nothing to sleep in."

"Where did you get it?" I ask, moving closer.

She edges back warily until she hits the wall. "I . . . erm . . . I found it."

"Where exactly?" I ask.

She looks past me. "In . . . in there."

I glance back to my room. "You went in my room?"

"I didn't look at anything," she rushes to add. "I just needed a shirt, and you were busy outside, so I—"

"Where were the dogs?" I demand.

She visibly swallows. "In my room."

I look around and notice they're not on the landing, so I grab her upper arm, causing her to wince, and shove her back into her room. I fill the doorway, setting my sights on my dogs curled up on the end of Tess's bed. "What the fuck?"

"They were crying outside your door, so I let them in my room."

Neither have bothered to lift their lazy, traitorous heads. "Heel," I yell, and they rush to their feet, almost knocking Tessa out the way. "Out," I snarl, and they leave the room. I slam the door and step farther into her room. "You went in my room," I repeat. She gives a slight nod. "Without my permission."

"You were busy," she almost whispers.

"And you took the opportunity to make yourself at home?"

"It's just a shirt," she murmurs.

"My shirt," I snarl, and she backs away, suddenly looking uncertain. "You're not here as a fucking guest."

"I know."

"Do you?" I ask, tipping my head to one side as I close the space between us. "You're wearing my shit, comforting my dogs . . . Jesus, you're even pleasuring yourself on my balcony like you ain't got a worry in the world." Her cheeks colour with embarrassment. "Take it off."

Her eyes shoot to mine. "Huh?"

"Take. It. Off."

"Pit," she tries to reason, but I have a dark desire to see her just once and it makes me a dick, but I never claimed to be anything other.

"Now." She sighs heavily before fixing me with a steely glare that makes me want to smile. She removes the shirt in one fast motion and shoves it hard against my chest. "Better," I whisper, trailing my eyes down her naked body. She's thinner than she should be, and I vow to feed her more while she's here. There are bruises down her legs from her encounter in the garden and they stand out against her pale skin. "Get on the bed."

She swallows hard and slowly drops back onto the bed, dragging herself farther up until she's resting against the headboard. I can see her inner turmoil—she wants to grab the sheets, but her stubbornness won't allow it. I take the armchair from the corner of the room, dragging it to the foot of the bed and taking a seat. "Why did you marry him?"

She rolls her eyes. "I thought you didn't care about all that? Aren't you killing me anyway, so what does it matter?"

"Call me curious."

"It was part of the agreement," she snaps, clearly not wanting to discuss it.

"Tell me the agreement."

"Why?"

I smirk. "Because if you don't, I'll take you back to the shack outside and leave you there for the night."

"I wanted security and stability in my life."

"You made the agreement?"

"What's wrong with that?" she snaps. "He gets something he wants, and I get something I need."

She's embarrassed, her cheeks are red, and she's defensive. She grabs the sheet and pulls it over herself. I allow it. "What exactly was he gonna pay for your virginity?"

"He's to transfer money into my account the day we fly out on our honeymoon. And he's also to support me like a husband would a wife throughout our marriage."

I rest my elbows on my knees, intrigued. "Tell me from the start."

She sighs again. "He contacted me after I advertised myself on a site—"

"There's a fucking site?" I cut in, unable to hide my shock. "Like virgins-dot-com?"

She rolls her eyes. "He asked to meet. We did and we hit it off."

"So, right now, you should be on your honeymoon?"

"Yes. We were leaving after the warehouse deal went through."

I grin. "Where was he taking you?"

She shrugs. "Dubai."

"And how much was that upfront fee he was supposed to transfer?"

"Five grand."

I almost choke on my own breath as I laugh loudly. She blushes deeper. "Five fucking grand? Whose idea was that?"

"His."

"I bet. Fuck, Tessa, five grand is nothing. You could've asked for a lot more."

"It wasn't just about the cash," she snaps, tugging the sheet higher and tucking it under her chin. "You wouldn't understand."

"And whose idea was the marriage?"

"Mine," she mutters. "I stated that on the site."

"What makes a girl like you need stability in the form of a stranger?" I ask, narrowing my eyes in wonder.

"What makes a man like you kill and kidnap?" she counters.

I arch a brow, smirking. "The money is good," I say honestly, "and I like it."

"Wow," she mutters, looking disgusted. "Do you get off on murdering people?"

"If I tell you my secrets, I'll definitely have to kill you."

She scoffs. "I thought that was already the plan."

"Maybe, maybe not. Why aren't you scared?" I ask, the question slipping from my lips before I have chance to stop it.

"Because when you live a life like mine, death is kinder."

Her words throw me. "What does that mean?"

"Forget it," she utters.

I grab the sheet and tug it hard, pulling it from her body. She doesn't react, instead just sighing patiently. "Your body was created for sin," I almost whisper, and her eyes dart to mine. "Touch yourself."

"Don't be absurd."

"Tessa," I say firmly, keeping eye contact, "touch yourself."

TESSA

I hesitate. The darkness in his eyes is daring me to follow his instruction, but my brain is screaming at me to wake the fuck up. This man is holding me against my will, and he knows I'm a virgin. If I encourage this, what does that make me? And what if he doesn't stop at teasing?

Fuck it. If I'm going to die, I may as well do the one thing the old me would never do and live a little.

I trail my fingers down my stomach, and his eyes follow them hungrily. I swipe a finger through my wetness and hiss, biting on my lower lip. I use my other hand to stroke my nipple, teasing the bud until it's hard before moving to the next. I close my eyes, enjoying the buzz it gives me to have a gorgeous man like Pit watching me.

The sound of his zipper has my eyes opening and my head shooting up. Pit is still sitting in the chair, but his hand is wrapped around his erection, which stands thick and proud. I still my fingers, staring as he moves his hand up and down his shaft.

I've never done this sort of thing, and I'm surprised how turned-on it makes me knowing I'm affecting him too. *Me*. It almost makes me feel powerful. I dip my fingers inside, gathering the wetness and rubbing it over my swollen clit. I work them faster as Pit does the same, panting as he chokes his cock in his hand with his eyes fixed between my legs.

I come hard, harder than I have before, and for the first

time ever, I think about sex. Hard, fast, dirty sex. *With him.* Pit stills his hand, and I watch as cum shoots out, hitting his shirt and dripping down his fist.

His head falls back and he stares at the ceiling while blindly wiping his mess using the T-shirt he took from me. After a few silent minutes, he tucks himself away and stands. "Sleep," he mutters, approaching me. He takes my hand and repeats his earlier taste test, licking my fingers clean. "I'd have paid five grand just to lick your pussy," he mutters before heading for the door.

I release a long breath, staring after him. *Fuck, he's hot.* My potential killer is HOT.

∽

THE NEXT MORNING, there's a sharp knock on the door, waking me from my slumber. I groan, rolling onto my back and rubbing my eyes. Memories of the early hours come flooding back, and I feel my cheeks heat. Now, I've got to face him.

"Breakfast is ready," says Pit, shoving my door open. His eyes trail over my bare legs sticking out from under the sheet. "You'll miss out if you're not quick. They're like savages down there."

"Your friends are still here?" I ask, feeling anxiety creeping in. "It's fine. I'll eat later."

His brow furrows. "You'll eat now."

How do I tell him that people terrify me? "Really, I'm happy up here, hidden away," I say, adding a little laugh to lighten the mood.

He steps into the room, watching me closely. "You

must be hungry. You've not had anything since breakfast yesterday."

"Well, that's your rule, isn't it? Feed me once a day?"

He goes over to the chair and picks up the T-shirt and bottoms he gave me to wear. He throws them my way. "I'll wait while you dress."

"Pit, I really don't want to go downstairs," I argue.

"There are other ways to make you, and I know they'll work." He arches a brow, and I sigh, pulling the clothes on.

"I'm not very good with people," I admit, my voice low.

"Me either."

"You don't understand," I push. "People tend to hate me. I'll say the wrong thing."

His brows are furrowed again as I ramble on, and then he does something odd—he holds out his hand, waiting for me to take it. After a few seconds staring at it, I stand and slide mine into his. "Take a breath," he orders, and I do. "It's going to be fine."

"Don't leave me," I mutter as we head for the door, and he glances back. "Please," I add. Because right now, I'm going with better the devil you know.

We enter the kitchen, where the large table is surrounded by people. It makes me want to vomit, even more so when their chatter dies down and they all glance our way. Pit keeps hold of my hand, leading me to the worktop and away from the table. I appreciate it. From this angle, I can back myself into the corner and just watch everyone else interact.

"Pancakes?" Pit asks, and I nod, but when he goes to step away, I immediately grab onto his arm. He pauses, glancing down where my fingers dig into his flesh, and I wince, releasing him immediately. "Tessa," he murmurs, turning to face me and blocking everyone's view, "I'm literally taking a few steps to get you some food. I'm not leaving you."

I give a stiff nod, and he steps back, holding eye contact. When he reaches the table, he quickly grabs a plate and loads it with pancakes and crispy bacon before returning to me and placing the plate on the worktop. "Eat," he whispers close to my ear.

"You have a lot of friends," I mutter, picking off a piece of fluffy pancake and stuffing it in my mouth.

Pit smirks. "Family," he corrects, and I arch a surprised brow. "These are my brothers."

"Brothers?" I repeat. "Your poor mother."

This makes him laugh, and I smile as he throws his head back, the sound radiating around us. "Not by blood, Te. My chosen family. My chosen brothers. And these are only a few—there's another thirty-odd back at the clubhouse."

"Clubhouse?"

"You never heard of bikers before, Tessa?" he asks. "It's a brotherhood of men who devote their lives to their club." There's a spark in his eyes when he mentions them, showing that deep down somewhere, he's got a heart.

I watch the group chatting. "And the women?"

He smirks again. "Club whores."

I almost choke. "Huh?"

"Ebony, London, Foxy, Jai," he tells me, pointing to each of the women as he says their names. "They work for the club."

"Doing what?"

He sniggers. "Anything the men ask of them, but mostly fucking and sucking cock."

I gasp and feel my cheeks colour with awkward embarrassment. "They like doing that?"

He shrugs. "I guess." Then he shouts to Ebony, and she saunters over, her eyes full of heat as she holds Pit's attention. "You enjoy fucking the guys?" he asks her, and my cheeks burn brighter.

"I especially enjoy fucking you, Pit," she says, tapping her pointy nail against his chest. "Why?"

"Tessa was asking."

She turns her eyes to me, and I shake my head back and forth. "I . . . no. He just said . . ." I stumble over my words, and she narrows her eyes in annoyance.

"Fuck, are you stupid or something?" She adds a shrill laugh.

Her words take me right back to school, and I shake my head harder. "No . . . I'm sorry, I just . . ."

She laughs harder, earning the attention of some of the others. "Oh my god, Pit, is this the whore you're replacing me with?"

"Don't be a bitch," says Pit, rolling his eyes.

"Look at her, she can't even string a sentence together. I . . . me . . . ermmmm." She breaks out in another round of laughter. "Suddenly, I'm not worried. You'll be back in my bed before the end of the week." She cackles as humiliation swallows me. I push past her and run for the back door, which is wide open. I almost stumble when my bare feet hit the stones, but it doesn't hurt as much as the humiliation of having a roomful of people laugh at me, so I ignore the pain as they cut my feet and I keep running.

CHAPTER 6

PIT

"Jesus, Ebony, what's your fucking problem?" I snap, shoving her away from me and following Tessa to the door. She's already stumbling down the garden path. I sigh in irritation. "Now, look what you've done."

"You want me to send a prospect after her?" asks Grizz, coming up behind me.

"Nah, I'll do it. She won't get far."

"She's a fucking drip," snaps Ebony. "She was practically crying like a baby."

"Don't be a cow," mutters London.

I stride up the path, watching as Tessa slows to a walk as she crosses the meadow that lies beyond the farm. She trails her hands out by her sides, letting the wildflowers tickle her fingers. "Yah know, there're grass snakes out here," I call after her.

She pauses, glancing back. "I'll take my chances."

"I could always whistle for the dogs," I add. Her shoulders slump and she stops walking. I close the distance between us. "She's a bitch. Ignore her."

"I told you I wasn't good with people."

"Tessa, that wasn't you. It was her being intimidating. She preys on . . ." I trail off.

"The weak," she mumbles.

"No, that's not what I meant."

"It's fine. I am weak. Girls like her," she sighs, shrugging, "I'm just not like her."

I place my hands on her shoulders, and we both stare out over the field. "That's not a bad thing," I tell her.

"I should be able to handle women like her," she says, her voice laced with anger. "But I can't. It doesn't matter how old I get, I just can't. I freeze up. And with all the practise I've had, it shouldn't be so hard."

"You were bullied?" I guess.

"Most of my life," she admits.

I shouldn't care, but her words make my heart ache for her. "Let's get back to the house. I'll make sure Ebony keeps her distance."

She shakes her head. "You go. I want to sit out here a while."

I smirk. "Nice try, Te."

She turns to me, rolling her eyes and sighing. "Where am I going to go?" she asks. "It's just fields. I won't run. Get King out here to babysit."

I grab her by the hand and continue forward until we get to a clearing and I sit down. "I'll stay out here with you for a while. You could do with some sunshine on that pale face."

After a few seconds, she lowers beside me. "Thanks."

"School was shit for me," I tell her. "I wasn't bullied, but I just didn't fit. Me and rules don't get on."

She smiles and her whole face lights up. It's almost as cute as when she comes. "I can imagine."

"Bullies are usually making up for something lacking in their own lives."

She scoffs. "If you knew how many times I've heard that."

"Doesn't make it better," I guess, and she shakes her head. "And now, you're here with me." She nods again. "It doesn't have to be all bad." Her eyes meet mine. "We don't have to make it harder by fighting all the time."

"You're gonna kill me."

"It hasn't been decided officially," I say with a shrug.

She scoffs. "If your boss called you right now and gave you the go-ahead, you'd do it."

I run my tongue over my lower lip and stare out across the horizon. "It's just how shit works in my world."

"It doesn't have to."

"It does, Te. No loose ends."

"I'm not a loose end, Pit. I'm an actual person with feelings."

Up until last night, it's not how I've allowed myself to think of her. When she was just the enemy, a threat to me, it was easier. But now, I've seen her come, I've tasted her, and I've seen her fear and want to irradicate it. If she was to name every person who bullied her, I'd have no problem teaching them a lesson.

"How?" she asks, breaking my thoughts. When I look at her blankly, she adds, "Are you going to do it?"

Slitting her throat was the obvious choice, but I don't tell her that. "How do you want me to?"

She pouts thoughtfully, picking at the blades of grass beside her thigh. "I've never thought about it. Something quick," her eyes light up, "or in my sleep." She nods as if confirming that to herself. "Yes, in my sleep."

"It's not a fucking fairy tale," I utter.

"I could swallow pills or something."

I roll my eyes. "Everyone assumes that's a quick death, to fall to sleep and never wake up. It's bullshit. You're in agonising pain, like rolling around on the bed screaming, and nine times out of ten, you'll vomit, bringing half the pills back up. Then you'll be left with irreversible damage to your organs and probably die a slow, painful death."

She's staring at me wide-eyed. "How do you know?"

"It's my job to know, Te. You want quick, I can give you quick, but it won't be pills."

"What do you recommend?"

I laugh. "You know, this is the strangest conversation I've ever had."

"I don't suppose you talk to your victims before you kill them," she says thoughtfully.

"Never," I confirm. "But if it was me, I'd want a knife straight to the heart."

She winces. "No."

"It's quick. After the initial shock wears off, your heart just stops pumping."

"Again, no," she says. "When I go to heaven, I want my heart intact."

"Heaven?" I repeat. "What makes you think that exists?"

She shrugs, going back to pulling up the grass. "I have to hold on to something, right? A beautiful afterlife that's different to here," she continues. "Better."

"No bullies?" I guess.

She nods. "And nobody wanting to use me or hurt me." She sighs. "Sounds like bliss."

I glance back to the farm and notice Grizz watching us from the doorway as he sucks on a cigarette. "We need to go back," I tell her, standing and holding out my hand for her. She eventually slips her hand into mine, and the familiar buzz in my heart hums louder. I pull her to her feet, and she winces, lifting one foot. "You're hurt?"

"It's nothing," she says, waving me away.

"Let me see," I say firmly, crouching before her. She holds onto my shoulder and lifts her foot. It's bleeding where stones have sliced into her skin. I tap her other ankle, and she lifts it, revealing it's the same. "Don't ever fucking run like that again, Te. You get upset, you squeeze my hand and I'll take you away from it, okay?" I look up, and she's staring with her sad blues calling to me. I stand, and her eyes follow me as I tip her head back to keep contact. "Is that clear?" I push.

"Yes," she almost whispers.

"Good. Glad we understand one another." I scoop her into my arms, and she yelps in surprise as I carry her back towards the house.

I march past Grizz and the rest of the brothers and head upstairs, not stopping until we're in my bedroom. I didn't even think about where to take her, and as I sit her on the edge of the bed, I try not to read too much into it. I go into my cupboard and retrieve the first aid kit, laying it open beside her. "Thanks," she mutters, dipping her hand in to take a bandage.

I crouch in front of her, aware this is the second time I've been on my knees for this woman. I take the bandage from her and place it back, retrieving an antiseptic wipe instead. I lift her left foot and begin to wipe it clean, gently removing debris and small stones, then I move to the next and do the same. "We need to find you some shoes," I say, taking the cream from the kit and applying it to the cuts. "Why were you barefoot anyway?"

"I took off my heels when I saw you come into the warehouse."

I glance up. "You must've been scared that night." She nods, and I feel a pang of guilt. She never asked to be in this situation. "If it's any consolation, we didn't plan on finding anyone there, especially not you."

"I won't tell anyone," she says, keeping her eyes to the ground.

I push to stand, sighing heavily. "You say that now, Te, but what about when the police come asking about Alec, or your family and friends want to know where you've been?"

"I don't have any," she says, finally looking at me. "I don't have anyone." I find it hard to believe her, she's lied too many times, and besides, she'd said her family would be worried. As if she's read my mind, she adds, "I lied before."

"You do that a lot."

"I was scared for my life, Pit. I'd have said anything to make you think twice about taking me."

"But this time is different, right?"

"Yes," she says eagerly. "You weren't after me, and Alec stole from you, so I get it. But this was nothing to do with me, and you can trust me to keep it quiet."

"I don't even know you," I spit, and she recoils slightly.

"You watched me . . . yah know, touch myself."

I laugh. "And now we're besties? Newsflash, Tessa, I've seen women come more times than I've had hot dinners. Your wet pussy is the same as the next bird's, and the one after that."

Her cheeks turn pink in that sexy, innocent way she's got, and I fight the urge to push her back onto my bed and taste her. "Is Ebony one of them?" she questions, and I almost laugh. She's seriously fucking asking me who I've fucked.

"Yep, and London, and Foxy, and even Siren before Grizz got his hands on her. I've fucked all the whores, Tessa." She stands, wincing again, and I shove her back onto the bed. "Not so fast, I haven't finished."

I crouch back down and take a bandage, ripping the package open and carefully wrapping it around her foot. "It's a little excessive," she mutters, folding her arms over her chest. "It's just a few grazes." I ignore her, wrapping her other foot too. "For the record, I think it's disgusting. You clearly don't respect women."

I place my hands either side of her thighs and crowd her, pushing my face to hers. "For the record, I don't give a shit what you think."

"You're a pig, using women and referring to them as whores."

"You heard Ebony yourself, she loves it. She loves me."

"But you don't feel the same," she spits angrily. "You use her, giving her false hope."

"You don't know shit about me, Tessa. She might be my one true love."

"So, why were you watching me? Why did you lick my fingers?" Her words tumble out, and she instantly reddens.

I smirk, brushing my nose against hers. She inhales sharply. "Because I could." Her eyes dart down to my lips, and I feel her breaths coming in sharp, rapid bursts. "Go back to your room, Tessa. I'll come and get you later."

TESSA

I must have fallen asleep because when I wake, the sky is turning a deep shade of orange. I check my watch—it's almost seven in the evening.

Pit told me to stay in the room, but I'm thirsty and I need to pee. I go to the French doors and listen outside. There's no sign of laughter or talking, so maybe everyone left. The thought pleases me. I feel much more relaxed when it's just me and Pit.

I go to the bathroom before heading downstairs, and it's not until I step into the kitchen that I realise the women are still here but there's no sign of Pit or any of the men. My step falters, but it's too late to back out unnoticed as all three women have turned. London stands, smiling kindly. "Pit went to tell you that he needed to head out, but you were sleeping. He shouldn't be too long. Are you hungry?" I shake my head, folding my arms over my chest. I turn to go back the way I came but stop when she adds. "Don't leave. Join us."

"I shouldn't," I mutter.

"Pit said not to do this," hisses Ebony, tugging London's arm.

London shrugs her off. "I don't give a shit. She's been up there for hours. She must be hungry."

"It's not our concern," Ebony pushes. "Go back to your room," she tells me.

"No," snaps London. "Ignore Ebony, she's not in charge. I'm London." She holds out a hand for me to shake, and I do so. "We hang around The Chaos Demons," she adds.

"Servicing their every need," adds Foxy, winking.

"I'm going to get the prospect," snaps Ebony, but London blocks her path.

"Sit the fuck down and stop being such a bitch. Pit will never get with you, so get over it." Ebony sits down, huffing loudly. "Ignore her, she's a jealous cow," London whispers, and we share a smile. "Where are you from?"

"Nottingham originally," I say. "I moved here when I was a teenager."

"Nice. A few of the Demons are from that way. Are you married, kids?"

It's such a normal conversation, but it's so out of place here. I give a stiff nod. "Married."

"I can't wait to get married," she says wistfully, sitting at the table and patting the space beside her so I'll do the same.

"No one's gonna marry you, London. Not from the club anyway," says Ebony, rolling her eyes.

I shift uncomfortably. Sitting with these women feels so foreign to me. It's not that I've never had friends. In school, I was quiet, but I had a few close friends who were the same as me. They went off to university, and we lost touch. When I began to work, I made friends with people in my team, but again, it was the quietest ones, and we never met up outside of work or anything. I've never really fit in anywhere.

I tune back in to the conversation as London is listing the reasons men love her. "You're forgetting your snatched vagina," adds Foxy, laughing. She turns to me. "She paid to have it tightened."

I gasp, and London smirks. "It was worth every penny."

"Yeah, and then Pres didn't even bother to sample it because he met Lexi," Ebony points out.

"He missed out," says London, laughing. She nudges shoulders with me. "Tell us about your man."

"London," Ebony hisses, "this isn't going to go down well with Pit or the VP."

"Relax," says London. "We won't tell them." She smiles warmly at me. "Go on."

"Nothing to tell, really. It was a bit of a shotgun wedding actually."

She gasps. "Oh shit, are you pregnant?"

I shake my head. "No, nothing like that. I didn't marry for love." London's smile fades, and I stare at the tabletop to avoid her pity. "It was a mutual thing."

"Did you want to get married?" asks Foxy.

I nod. "It was my idea. Well . . . it was part of the deal."

"Deal?" Ebony repeats, suddenly looking interested.

"We need details," London cuts in. "Give me tips on how to get a man to marry me."

I almost smile. "It was stupid really," I mutter, suddenly feeling embarrassed. "I got drunk and signed up to a dating app."

"Oh my god, I love a dating app," London gushes.

"I wasn't looking to date. I wanted a husband."

"So, you just put that in your bio?" asks Ebony, smirking.

"Yeah," I say. "I was offering something all men want . . . apparently."

"What?" they ask in unison.

"My virginity."

They all stare wide-eyed. "You're a virgin?" asks London, looking impressed.

"Of course, she is," says Ebony, rolling her eyes.

"Hey, do you reckon I could say the same?" asks London.

Foxy laughs. "Please, girl, even with the snatch job, you're still looser than a prostitute's mouth."

"I'm not making it up," I say. "I am a virgin."

"How?" asks London, looking confused.

"I just didn't meet the right man."

"Where were you hiding, under a rock?" asks Ebony.

"I worked long hours and didn't socialise much."

"Let me get this straight. You lived like a nun, joined a dating app, and asked for marriage in exchange for your V-card?" asks London. I nod, and she laughs, holding up her hand for us to high-five. I do, even though I feel uncomfortable. "Good for you."

"Hold on," says Foxy. "You said you *are* a virgin. Didn't you go through with the deal?"

"Not exactly. We got married, but Alec had one last job to do before we went on our honeymoon, and then I got brought here."

The women exchange wary looks. "You should go upstairs before he comes back," says Foxy, and the others nod in agreement.

I stand, and London places her hand over mine. "I like you, Tessa. I hope we see you again."

CHAPTER 7

PIT

Axel bangs the gavel on the table and the brothers fall silent. "How's things with the girl?" he asks me.

"Same," I say with a shrug. "I've left her in London's capable hands. She's not had friends before, so I reckon she might open up to her."

He gives a nod. "Good idea." He slides her mobile across the desk. "No tracker. Maybe he didn't get time to fit it."

I take it. "He's not been in touch?"

Axel shakes his head. "Get the girl to call him. I wanna know what he's got to say. If he isn't bothered about her, there's no point in us keeping her around."

"Pres," snaps Coop, and Axel holds his hand up.

"I don't wanna hear it, Coop. She's no good to us, and what the fuck am I meant to do with her? Pit wants to get back on the road. He don't wanna babysit."

I nod in agreement, even though right now, I want nothing more than to babysit. Something about her makes me want to be around her. I spent an hour this afternoon watching her fucking sleep. *Sleep.* I'm going soft.

"Alec knows we've got a shitload of stock stored at the docks. He might strike again. I've had to put more men on the yard cos we don't stand a chance of moving it," says Grizz.

"Until we speak to him and find out what he wants, or until we end him, we'll just have to pay for the extra men," says Axel. "But it's coming out of everyone's subs." The brothers groan, and Axel slams the gavel on the table. "Get the fuck out of here."

We wait for the room to clear as I sit back at the table with Axel and Grizz. "How long we giving this?" I ask.

"A few days?" suggests Grizz, looking to Axel for confirmation.

"Yeah, three max." I nod stiffly and rise to my feet.

"Look, I'm with Coop on this, and I hate hurting innocent women—women full stop, to be honest—so if there's another way to keep her quiet, just say the word," adds Axel.

I head for the door. There is no other way. Unless we can strike a deal that satisfies Alec and the club, Tessa will die.

∼

LONDON CHEWS on her lower lip, eyeing me as I pour myself a whiskey. "Did she suspect?" I ask, sitting on a rock closest to the fire.

"No. Although Ebony was a cow and almost had her running back to her room. She didn't say much, just what you already know about the dating app. I'll keep trying." I nod. "In the meantime, if you need your bed kept warm . . ." She trails off, leaving the sentence open.

I run my eyes over her bronzed body and give a slight nod. "Wait in my room," I tell her.

She stands gracefully, walking towards me and bending slow to place a lingering kiss on my lips. I close my eyes. "I can't wait," she whispers, walking away. I open them again to see Tessa sitting on the balcony watching us. Guilt fills me, though fuck knows why. I haven't done anything wrong.

I knock the whiskey back and place the glass on the grass by my feet. Then I stand and head after London.

I stop outside my room with my hand on the doorknob, but before I can go inside, Tessa's door opens. She steps out, staring at me expectantly. Her chest rises and falls fast, like her heart is racing, and then she tugs her lower lip between her teeth.

The silence stretches out between us, and then my hand falls away from the doorknob and I stride towards her, closing the gap in seconds. Our mouths crash together hungrily, and her arms wrap around my neck as I lift her into my arms, pulling her against me as I back into her bedroom and kick the door closed.

Sliding her down my body, I run my hands up her sides, lifting her T-shirt and pulling it from her body, dropping it to the ground. We don't break the kiss as I push her back onto the bed and crawl over her body. My cock strains in my jeans as I move my mouth across her cheek and along her collarbone. Her hands grip my shoulders, and she closes her eyes as I circle her nipple with my tongue. It puckers, and I close my lips over it, gently tugging.

As I move down her body, her legs fall open and I settle between them. She stills, realising my mouth is inches from her pussy, and when I run my tongue through her wetness, she gasps. I press my thumb over her swollen clit, and she arches her back. "You ever been touched like this before, Te?" I ask.

TESSA

His voice comes out strained, rumbling through me and causing shivers in my core. "No," I whisper, "not like this." He swipes his tongue again, and I push my fingers into his hair, tugging him closer.

I forced myself to step out into the hallway. I didn't want him going into his room, where I knew London was waiting for him. I didn't analyse why, because I knew I'd talk myself out of it, but for once, I'm living a little. If this is my last few weeks or days on this earth, then I'm going to have sex. *I will not die a virgin.*

Pit keeps the pressure on my clit, occasionally licking along my opening and humming his approval. I feel a warmth building, way more intense than when I touch myself. "You look fucking hot," he murmurs.

Sparks burst and my insides melt into mush as I shudder, clinging to his hair and panting as the convulsions take over. I loosen my grip on his hair, and my hands fall to my sides while I bask in the warmth, relaxing into the mattress.

Pit crawls back up my body, and I take a breath,

readying myself for whatever he plans to do now, but he surprises me by climbing from the bed. "Goodnight, Te."

I frown, glancing at the bulge in his jeans. "Aren't we going . . ."

He smirks. "Have sex?" I nod. "No, Tessa. Get some rest."

He heads for the door, and I stare after him in confusion. "Why?" I blurt out, unable to stop myself.

He pauses, his hand resting against the door frame. "You're bought and paid for, Te."

His words are like a bucket of ice water over me, and I instantly grab the sheet to cover myself. "I'm not a prostitute," I mutter.

"You're as good as," he mutters, stepping out. "Goodnight." Then he closes the door gently.

My heart twists painfully in my chest. I'm married. It's not like I've sold my virginity to the highest bidder on eBay.

I get off the bed and snatch my shirt from the floor, pulling it on. If that's how he feels, then fuck him. I begin to pace. Why do I care anyway? He's a murderer, and he's holding me here against my will. I run my fingers through my hair in irritation. *Prick.* And now, what? He's gone to fuck a woman he actually refers to as a whore? I growl out loud. *I don't think so.*

Ripping the door open, I let it smash back against the wall and march towards his room. I pause at the sound of a woman moaning in pleasure. I ball my fists in anger and raise one, banging hard on the door. The sounds stop. "What?" he calls.

I scoff, shoving the door, and to my surprise, it opens.

Only London isn't spread on the bed being fucked. Pit smirks as I stare wide-eyed.

"Did you want something, Te?" he asks, his tone teasing. "Cos if not, I'm kinda in the middle of something." He presses play on the television remote, and my eyes glance at the woman on the screen, screaming as she fakes an orgasm. Then my eyes fall back to Pit, who's got his thick erection in his hand. "Te," he hisses, "are you coming in to watch or not?"

I should run. I should go back to my room and pretend like tonight never happened. But I step in farther and close the door. I can't deny it—I'm so attracted to him, I can't think straight.

He smirks, patting the space beside him. I go over like a lamb for slaughter, staring wide-eyed at the television. I'm too scared to look at Pit's erection as he strokes his hand up and down. "You done this before?" he asks, and I shake my head stiffly. "Relax, Tessa, no one's forcing you here. Leave if you want to."

I glance at him. "Show me what to do."

He reaches for my hand, and I willingly give it to him. He guides it to his cock, and I grip it, just like he had. His chest heaves heavily as he places his hand over mine and begins to move it. I turn slightly so I'm able to watch his face. His eyes are no longer on the screen but on me, and he slides his hand up my thigh and under my shirt. I've been without underwear since he took my panties to be washed, and as he brushes his fingers through my wetness, I realise I don't miss it.

The urge to kiss him is strong, so I boldly lean closer. He watches, waiting for me to make the move. I lightly brush my lips over his, tilting my head so I can deepen it. "I want to taste you," I whisper against his lips. He inhales sharply, watching with a surprised expression as I lower my head towards his cock. He releases my hand, letting me take control.

I lick my tongue over the end, and he groans. "All fours, Te," he mutters, tapping my thigh. I push onto my knees, keeping my backside near him so he can explore me with his fingers.

As he slides one finger into me, I envelop his erection with my mouth, swirling my tongue over the swollen head. "Suck," he pants, tangling his free hand into my hair. I take him deeper into my mouth, the weight of him pressing against my tongue as he brushes the back of my throat, making me gag. I jerk back, releasing him, and wipe my mouth on the back of my hand. Risking a glance at him, I find his eyes full of lust and fixed on me. "Do it again," he mutters, guiding my head back to his cock.

This time, I fight the urge to gag and close my eyes, breathing through my nose as I suck on him. His busy fingers use my wetness to glide over my clit, distracting me as the build-up of an orgasm looms. Pit begins to push on my head, and each time I suck him in, he urges me to take him deeper, until he's practically fucking my throat. "Te, I need to come," he pants, his voice urgent. His words spur me on, and I take him as far as my throat will allow, holding still as his grip tightens on my hair. "Fuckkkk," he murmurs on a groan, and then he stiffens and spurts of warm liquid hit my tonsils. I try to swallow as much as I can, but it's an impossible task and it spills from the corners of my mouth. He keeps my head held there while his body jerks.

When he finally releases me, I sit, using his discarded T-shirt to wipe my mouth. "That was fucking hot," he mutters, his breaths still shallow as the woman in the background continues to fight her way through another orgasm. "Let me return the favour," he offers, bringing my attention from the screen. I'm still reeling from what just happened as he grips my arm and tugs me to him. "Sit on my face."

I frown. "I can't . . . I might hurt you," I reply, embarrassed. It's not like I'm stick thin. I have curves, and in true woman style, I'm my biggest self-critic.

He smirks. "Sit. On. My. Face."

I move closer, realising he won't let this go, and I'm pretty sure the second I sit over him, he'll realise what a mistake it is and give up. I throw my leg over his chest, and he inches down until his mouth is level with my pussy. "Eyes on me," he orders, and I stare down in disbelief as he hooks his arms around my thighs and pulls me down onto him. I gasp when his tongue swipes along my opening. He keeps me firm against him while he tortures my clit with slow licks. His thumb presses against me, and I shudder. "Don't come," he says, withdrawing his attention. He slides me down his body until I'm sitting over his cock. I glance down, and even in its semi-hard state, it's big.

I swallow my nerves. The time has come to bite the bullet and just give it up. I've held onto my virginity for far too long in the hope of finding true love, and when that failed, I sold it to a man who led me here, into this mess.

"Relax, Te, we ain't fucking," says Pit, his voice

breaking my racing thoughts. He pushes me to sit against him, my pussy pressed against his cock as it lays flat along his stomach. He grips my hips hard enough to leave finger bruises, but I welcome them as he guides me to slide against him. A thrill shoots through me as my clit rubs against his cock. He slides his hands up my body until he's teasing my nipples, urging me to move faster and chase my release.

I come hard, jerking against him as the warmth rolls through my body. "Hot," he murmurs, cupping the back of my neck and pulling me to meet his lips. He kisses me until my orgasm passes, and I collapse against him. I feel wetness between us and realise he came again, and it's all over his stomach. Wrapping me in his arms, he gently strokes his fingers up and down my spine. "So fucking hot," he mutters, ignoring the mess we've made.

∾

I WAKE to the smell of food and stretch out. I open my eyes and memories of last night come flooding back. Sitting upright, I look around, realising I'm still in Pit's bed. I glance down at my naked body and immediately scramble to pick up my clothes. The door opens and Pit appears holding a wooden tray. He smiles, and I pause as he kicks the door closed behind him. "I made breakfast," he says, ignoring the fact I'm half stood up with the T-shirt hanging around my neck. "Get back into bed."

I do it, sticking my arms through the shirt as I sink back. I'm not sure if I follow his orders because I want to or because, deep down, I know he's in charge. My future is in this man's hands, and I don't want to rock the boat.

He slips into bed and places the tray in the centre. I stare at the pile of freshly picked strawberries along with two hot croissants. "The jam is homemade," he tells me proudly, and I frown. How can this man, who I watched kill someone, make fucking jam? He continues to split a croissant in half before lathering it in the sticky goodness and holding it out to me, unaware of the inner turmoil I currently face. "Go on, try it," he urges, nodding.

I take it, and he watches with anticipation as I take a bite. It's good. Probably the best I've ever tasted. I give a nod, but still, he stares, and eventually, I ask, "What?"

"That's it, just a nod?"

"What do you want me to say?"

"The truth. Is it good or not?"

"You know it is," I say. "It's amazing."

He leans back against the headboard with a satisfied smile on his face. "Good."

We eat in silence. I finish the pastry, and he forces the second half on me, insisting I eat it all. I refuse the strawberries as I haven't eaten properly for days and my stomach is surprisingly full. Pit moves the tray to the bedside table, taking a strawberry from the pot and holding it to my lips. "Just one bite," he says.

I take a bite, feeling the juice drip down my chin. Before I can wipe it, he runs his tongue there, gathering it and pressing his lips to mine in a bruising kiss. He's intoxicating, and I could easily get lost, but his hand travels under my shirt and cups my breast, snapping me from my lustful thoughts. I pull back, and he pops the rest of the strawberry into his mouth.

"I should shower," I mutter.

"Why are you looking like that?" he asks, grabbing the television remote and turning it on to a news channel. He mutes it and turns to look at me, waiting for my reply. I shrug. "Like you're scared or some shit."

"I am."

He arches a brow. "Of me?"

"Yes."

"Even though just a few hours ago, you sat on my face then masturbated against my cock?" My cheeks burn instantly, and I stare down at the floor. "Take the shirt off," he adds. I go to remove it, but he places a hand over mine, stilling me. "Take it off because you want to, not because I've ordered you to." I remove it, dropping it to the floor. "When we're alone like this, you should always be naked," he says, pulling me to lie back and trailing his mouth over my stomach and up to my breasts. "When we're like this, let's forget all the shit that got us here and pretend none of that exists."

I close my eyes, letting his magic hands take me to another place, allowing my mind to do exactly what he's suggested and pretend that nothing else exists outside of this moment. I push away the doubts I have about his sanity, and the worrying signs staring me in the face over his split personality. One minute, he's got me by the throat, and the next, he's making fucking jam. If it wasn't so fucked-up, it'd be funny.

CHAPTER 8

PIT

"Did you get her to call him?" asks Axel.

"No answer, Pres," I say. It's easier to lie over the phone when he can't see it on my face. "I'll keep trying."

The truth is, I haven't even raised the topic with Tessa yet, and right now, I don't want to. The house is still full of brothers who are taking turns to show up here and keep me company, ensuring the road doesn't call to me. So, I split my time between them and her, sneaking off to the room whenever I can and spending the nights beside her, making her come. When I'm with her, everything else fades away, including the nagging desire to hit the road. We don't even fucking talk. We touch each other like teenagers exploring for the first time, but no words pass unless they're words of encouragement from me as she explores what she likes.

"And things are good?" Axel asks, bringing me back to the call.

"Grizz reckons you're keeping her under lock and key."

"Ain't that the idea of a prisoner?" I ask.

"Sure, as long as that's what she is."

I frown. "What are you asking me, Pres?"

He sighs heavily. "I don't even know," he mutters, "but, Pit, whatever is happening with you two, don't let it go too far."

I bristle at his words. It always was hard to pull the wool over his eyes. "What are you talking about?"

"Don't fuck her, Pit," he says firmly. "Whatever happens, don't fuck her. She's bought and paid for, and if we let her walk, he'll want her in the exact condition she was."

His words are like ice-cold water being thrown over me. She belongs to *him*. "You're way off, Pres." I force the words to leave my mouth before disconnecting the call. I slam the mobile on the table and clench my fists as jealousy courses through me. It's not like it wasn't in the back of my mind already. That's the reason I haven't fucked her, cos lord knows I've wanted to. The thoughts of sinking into her wake me through the night, which usually leads to me waking her so I can fuck her mouth.

I hear footsteps padding across the floor, and before I turn, arms wrap around my waist, and I instantly know it's her. I immediately pull away and glance at the window to see my brothers sitting around the firepit. "What are you doing down here?" I snap.

She takes a step back. "Sorry, I was thirsty."

"Then you go to the bathroom and drink water," I say

coldly. The last thing I need is Grizz seeing us together and witnessing shit between us. "Go back upstairs."

"Pit, are you coming outside?" I turn to the sound of London's voice as she appears in the doorway.

"I'll be right there," I say.

She leans against the doorframe, her eyes running back and forth between us. "Tessa, it's been a few days since I saw you. Are you okay?"

"Fine," Tessa mutters.

"She was just going back upstairs," I say coldly.

"Why don't you join us?" asks London.

"Because she's not here for fun," I interject.

Tessa brings her eyes to me, arching a brow. "Just when it suits, right?" And she spins on her heel and heads back upstairs.

London moves closer, pushing the door closed. "Okay, what was that?"

"Nothing," I mutter.

"Didn't sound like nothing, Pit. Are you and her—"

"Of course not," I snap, cutting off her words. "She's got it in her head she likes me. Probably that fucking syndrome."

"Stockholm?" she asks, and I nod.

"Perhaps let the Pres know," she says, eyeing me warily, and I know she hasn't bought my bullshit. "Yah know, just so he's in the loop."

I step to her, tucking her hair behind her ear, "No need," I tell her. "I've got it under control." I place a kiss to her head and move around her, heading out to join my brothers.

IT'S ALMOST three in the morning by the time I stumble upstairs. I open my door to find my bed empty. I'm surprised how pissed that makes me as I stalk towards Tessa's room and shove the door open to find her curled up in the centre of the bed, sleeping soundly. I march over and scoop her up in my arms. She immediately wakes, and I hate that she's on high alert, like she's just waiting for something bad to happen.

"Relax," I whisper, nuzzling my nose into her hair. "It's just me."

I carry her to my room and dump her on my bed. She sits up, bringing her knees to her chest. "I don't want to sleep in here with you," she mutters, eyeing me warily as I get undressed.

I shouldn't force the issue. She's giving me an out here. I could let her go back to her room, stop this fucking insane need I have to sleep beside her, and get on with my job. Instead, I climb into bed and turn the bedside lamp out. "Go to sleep, Tessa."

I hear her move and then the sheets rustling, and I smile to myself, thinking she's following my orders. But then her lamp turns on and illuminates the room once again. I sigh heavily. "Why?" she asks.

"Why what?"

"Why do you want me in here with you?"

"It's what you want too," I say, closing my eyes in the hope she'll follow my lead.

"Bullshit, Pit. I'm so fucking confused."

When I open my eyes, she's resting her forehead on

her knees like she's exhausted. "Why have we got to question it and pull it apart, Te? Let's just enjoy it."

"While it lasts?" she questions, turning her head to the side so she can see me. "Because I can't do this anymore, Pit. I lie beside you, wondering if tonight will be the night that you," she swallows hard, "kill me."

"We're waiting on your man to come rescue you."

She gives an empty laugh. "He isn't fucking coming, is he? If he was, he'd have been in contact by now."

"He paid a lot of money," I say, the words turning my stomach. "He'll come for you."

"And when he does, then what?"

"We'll cross that bridge when we come to it."

"See," she snaps, throwing her feet over the edge of the bed and standing. "I know what will happen—you'll kill him for taking your stuff, and then you'll kill me. I'm the fucking bait, right?"

When I don't answer, she heads for the door, but before she's even touched the handle, I'm out of bed and grabbing her around the waist. I hold her to me, pressing my nose to her hair and inhaling. "Just give me more time," I whisper, not really knowing what the fuck I mean, just knowing I need her to stay. "I'll work it out."

"What does that mean?"

"It means give me more time," I grit out.

"Are you and London . . ." Her words trail off, and I feel her relax into me.

"No," I say firmly. "It's just you."

She turns in my arms. "Really?"

I nod, brushing hair from her face. "Now, please, come

to bed." She gives a slight nod, and I relax, taking her hand and leading her back.

Once she's settled against my chest, I close my eyes.

"Pit?" They shoot open again. "How did you get the scar?" She runs her fingers over the jagged scar that runs across my cheek.

"A piece of glass," I tell her, allowing my eyes to shut once more while she continues to touch my face.

"Who did it?"

I smirk. "Did you have a nice childhood, Tessa?"

"Not really. You?"

I shake my head, and her hand falls from my scar and rests against my chest. "No. My mum cut my face."

I feel her stiffen slightly. "Why?"

"Because she was off her face on drugs and thought I was the devil." I laugh. "Maybe she was right."

"How old were you?"

"Eight."

"Jesus. Did you get taken from her?"

"No, Te. I didn't tell anyone."

She cranes her head back to look at me. "Why?"

"Because she was my mum."

"Did she hurt you again?"

I run my fingers through her hair. "More times than I care to remember."

"I'm really sorry, Pit."

I kiss the top of her head. "Don't be. It was a long time ago, and it made me stronger."

"No kid deserves that."

"What about you?" I ask. "Where did you grow up?"

"In the countryside at first, then we moved because of Dad's job. It was a council estate, not a good one."

"Both parents?"

"In the beginning. Mum died when I was little. My dad raised me."

"What'd she die of?" I ask.

"A broken heart," she says, her voice laced with sadness. "If you asked him, he'd say that was stupid, that you couldn't die from that, but she did."

"Your dad broke her heart?"

"He broke her completely. Body, mind, soul. He beat her down until she was nothing but an empty shell."

"It's a shit thing to live with as a kid, ain't it? Broken parents who hate each other so much, yet they can't be apart."

"She wouldn't leave," says Tessa. "Even though she hated how he treated her, she stayed for me. And when he realised that, he got a lot worse." We fall silent, and then she throws her leg over mine and pulls herself to sit over me. "Let's just forget about all that," she says, leaning down to kiss me.

TESSA

I wake the same as I have the last few mornings, with Pit bringing me breakfast in bed. Once we've eaten, and he's joined me in the shower, cleaning me mainly with his mouth, he takes me back to the bedroom, where some clothes have been laid out. "I got London to pick you up some things," he says, looking unsure. "I don't know if it's your style, but London seemed to think it would suit you."

I pick up the pair of jeans and hold them out. "They're great, thanks," I say with a smile. After days of wearing Pit's shirts, I'm looking forward to being clothed fully. I pick up a fitted T-shirt. It's something I'd usually wear, so I smile, adding it to the jeans hanging over my arm.

"In the bag, there's some new underwear. We went off the sizes on your others."

I peek inside and smile. There's a lot of underwear, mostly lace. "Thank you."

"And trainers," he adds, nodding to the floor where some brand-new Nikes sit. "Maybe you can get out into the garden?"

I nod eagerly, wanting to stretch my legs beyond these four walls. "I'd love to."

"Okay, get dressed and join me downstairs. We can take the dogs for a walk."

By the time I head down, Pit is waiting with both dogs sitting at his feet. King wags the second he spots me, and I smile, knowing I've won him over completely. Gigi, not so much, but I'm working on it.

Pit hands me a tennis ball. "They love this," he says as he heads for the door, whistling for the dogs to follow. I fall into step beside him, and he slips his hand in mine, leading me up the garden path and towards the field at the back of the farmhouse. The dogs run around my feet, King barking, eager for me to throw the ball, which I do, laughing as they rush off after it.

"You're not doing bad to say you hate dogs," says Pit, his tone teasing.

"I don't hate them. Well, not all dogs, just big ones . . .

and some small." I laugh again. "Okay, most dogs, but I have a history with them."

"Dogs are loyal, a man's best friend. The ones that are trained well don't attack for no reason."

"My dad kept big dogs," I admit, wondering where the need to tell him my life story seems to have come from. "He used them to keep us in line."

He side-eyes me. "That's fucked-up."

"Yeah. He was."

King drops the ball at my feet, and I scoop it up, throwing it again. "Why won't you have sex with me?" I blurt out, instantly regretting it when Pit stops and stares at me. "It's just, if you're going to kill me, I don't want to die a virgin." I don't add that he's driving me insane, and even though he always brings me to orgasm, sometimes even twice, I want him so badly, I'm dreaming of him.

"And what would your hubby have to say about that, Te?" he asks, smirking as he begins to walk again.

"So, you're handing me back to him?"

"I don't know," he mutters. "I told you, I'll come up with a plan."

"To set me free?"

"To try and keep everyone happy," he says, his tone irritated.

"But if your boss wants me dead then . . ."

Pit turns, pulling me against him and kissing me until my toes curl. When he pulls back, I'm panting. "I don't want to talk about it, Te. Let's not ruin the day."

∽

NICOLA JANE

BY THE TIME we get back to the house, I'm surprised none of Pit's friends are around. He indicates for me to sit at the table while he makes us a drink. When he joins me, I take the coffee gratefully. "Could you live here all the time?" I ask, looking around the kitchen. "It's so cosy."

He shrugs. "Not alone," he says eventually.

"Okay, if you found the right woman, would you stay here?"

He shrugs again. "I like the road."

"But you can't ride forever, right?"

He smirks. "I'll ride until my hips won't allow it."

"Haven't you ever wanted to just settle down?" I had dreams of finding *the one* so I could marry and have kids. I used to list baby names and wedding venues, even though I knew deep down it would never happen. Not for love, anyway, because who would love me? Then, the older I got, the more I realised kids weren't going to be part of my plan. I'd never want to put a child through the sort of things I've had to deal with. The world is too cruel.

"I never really thought about it," he admits. "I've always done what's best for the club."

"How did you even get into the club? Is it like a membership?"

He laughs, shaking his head. "No, Te, it's a brotherhood. I met Axel in prison a few years ago. He talked about the club like it was his entire life, and I thought, fuck, that's the kind of life I want. When I got out, I reached out. He's a good man, and he would lay his life down for any one of us."

"Sounds nice."

"It's a lifelong commitment, so if I settle down, my

woman has to be into that life too, and trust me, that's rare to find."

"What about London?" I ask, tapping my fingernail against the table.

He grins. "You're jealous."

"I'm not," I snap.

"London is a club whore, Te, just like Ebony and the others. They're not old lady material. At least, not mine."

"Why?"

"Because I don't want a woman all my brothers have fucked. I'm jealous, insanely so, and I want all her firsts." His words trail off as my heart slams hard in my chest. He stands abruptly, like he wants to erase what he just said, and pours his coffee down the sink. "You should go back upstairs before they get back," he says, placing his hands on his hips while keeping his eyes to the floor.

I feel my heart sink. Whenever I think we're getting somewhere, he shuts down and pushes me back up to the damn room. "Maybe we should try calling Alec," I suddenly suggest. If he gets jealous, he'll react to my suggestion, and that usually ends up with us in bed.

Instead, he scoffs. "Don't you think we've tried that?"

"Off my phone?" I question.

"Yes, Te, of course, off your phone."

"Then let me text him."

"He knows we have your mobile. He isn't responding."

"I have a codeword, so he'll know it's me," I say, and he narrows his eyes. "He had a nickname for me," I add, biting on my lower lip.

"A nickname?" he repeats, arching a brow.

I nod. "Firecracker."

Pit clenches his fists at his sides. "Go upstairs, Te."

"If I can get him out of hiding, you can sort it between yourselves and I can go."

He sniggers. "That's not how it works."

"Wouldn't you rather see me because I want to spend time with you, Pit?" I throw at him. "Instead of it being forced?"

"Room, now!" he bellows, and I jump in fright. The look in his eyes reminds me of how he would glare at me in the beginning, I haven't seen it for a while, and I forgot how much I dislike it.

"I hate you," I spit angrily as I head for the stairs.

He sneers. "Not enough to stop dry humping me though, sweetheart."

∼

I sit on the bed seething. I hate not knowing the plan, even though I'm pretty certain he'll never let me walk out of here alive. He's using me to lure Alec in, and it isn't working. Soon, he'll have no choice but to end me.

I bury my head in my hands and sigh heavily.

CHAPTER 9

PIT

I stand in the doorway watching as Axel's bike comes to a stop. He climbs off and removes his helmet. "Pres, this is a surprise," I say warily. He never comes out here and so far has only contacted me by phone.

"I wanna see the girl."

I arch a brow. "How come?"

He eyes me, narrowing them slightly. "Is there a problem?"

I shake my head. "No, Pres. I'll get her now." I head back inside. "Fuck," I mutter, taking the stairs two at a time. I burst into Tessa's room, and she spins to face me, half-dressed. She grabs her towel and holds it over herself. Since our disagreement two nights ago, she's refused to leave her room or even speak to me, which suits me fine. It's time we stopped fucking around anyway. Our time together is coming to an end.

"My Pres is here," I say.

"So?"

"So, you need to come down. He wants to see you."

She scoffs. "He isn't my President, so I don't have to do shit."

I close the distance between us, and she shrinks back slightly. "I ain't asking," I spit. "Get some fucking clothes on." She steps away, rolling her eyes but getting dressed. "He's gonna ask you some shit," I mutter, rubbing my hand over the back of my neck. "About Alec."

"I don't have any answers," she snaps.

"I told him we've been trying to call Alec." I feel her eyes on me. "And that he hasn't been picking up."

"But we haven't," she says, sounding confused.

"I know that," I say, my voice tight with irritation. "But I'd appreciate if you went along with it."

She laughs, not sounding amused. "You want me to cover up your lies?"

"Yes," I say stiffly.

"Why should I?"

"Because," I snap before taking a calming breath. "Because," I repeat more calmly, "I lied to buy you some time, to buy *us* some time." I let those words sink in, and a realisation passes over her face.

She heads for the door. "Fine."

Downstairs, Axel is sitting at the kitchen table with his hands braced together, resting on the solid oak. He points to the space opposite him, and Tessa lowers into it. "Your husband isn't coming out of hiding," he states.

"Maybe he doesn't give two shits about me," Tessa suggests, arching a brow.

"Where's her phone?" Axel asks, looking to me.

I go to the cupboard and retrieve it. Tessa stares wide-eyed, probably annoyed that her lifeline was easily accessible. I hand it to Axel, who turns it on. "When did you last try?"

I shrug. "A couple days ago."

His eyes narrow further, but he doesn't comment. He slides the handset towards Tessa. "Call him."

"I should text," Tessa replies. "Let him know it's really me."

Axel gives a nod, taking the phone back. "Tell me what to write."

"Firecracker," she replies.

Axel types it in and sends it, placing the phone back on the table. "Is there a reason you didn't try that before?"

Tessa smirks. "I don't like your man, so I've been difficult," she says, glancing at me with disgust.

"Maybe you're not as keen to get your freedom as I thought?" he asks.

"Oh, trust me, I want out of here."

"Good, because I'm taking you to the clubhouse tonight. Go and pack a bag."

Tessa's eyes find mine and she looks worried, though not as worried as me. I step forward. "Pres?" I ask.

"Now, Tessa," he says, dismissing her. Once she's gone, he turns to me, his cold expression in place. "It's for the best."

"Weren't we isolating her so the old ladies don't take her under their wing?"

"That's what you're worried about?" he asks, arching a brow with a slight smirk on his lips. "And here I was worrying you were gonna shag the captive." His smirk fades and he pushes to his feet. "Am I right?"

"It ain't like that," I begin, and he shoves me back, taking me by surprise, so I lose my footing.

"Don't fucking lie to my face, Pit. And you better not have touched her in any way that could compromise a potential deal." I don't quite meet his eyes, and he shoves me again, this time pressing me against the wall. "Reassure me, brother, before I have no choice but to lay into you."

"I haven't fucked her, Pres," I snap. "I wouldn't."

He releases me. "Keep it that way."

Tessa appears holding a plastic bag with her few belongings. "Is Pit coming?" she asks.

"No," says Axel bluntly. "Let's go."

"Wait," I say, and he pauses. "You're putting her on your bike?" The thought brings something out of me that'll get me into some serious shit with my Pres, but I can't let her go like this.

"Do you want to put her on yours?" He's challenging, and I know if I push too hard, he'll refuse point blank and probably lay into me just for fun.

"What about Lexi? She's your old lady. You can't just put another woman on your bike."

He knows I'm right, but he pulls out his mobile. "I'll speak to Lex."

"Or I could just bring her to the clubhouse," I suggest. He eyes me warily, and I hold my hands up. "She's already been on it, and I'll drop her at the club and leave."

"Fine," he mutters. "Let's go."

The second we pull away from the farm, her voice crackles through the speaker in my helmet. "Am I going to die tonight?"

"No, Te."

"How do you know?"

"Because that's my job and he hasn't ordered me to do it. He's going to keep us apart now."

"Why?"

"Because he knows."

"Knows what?"

I sigh heavily. "He knows what I want to do with you, Te. He can see it all over my face."

"And what do you want to do?"

I give a short laugh. "Oh baby, there is so much I wanna do, but you don't belong to me, so it's pointless even talking about it."

"You said before that you've been buying me time. What does that even mean?"

I realise there's no point lying to her. After this trip, I won't see her again. "Buying you more time on this earth," I mutter. "More time with me."

"So, now what?" she whispers.

"Just pray your man calls that phone, Te."

"I was scared to be with you, Pit," she murmurs, "but I'm terrified to be without you."

My heart aches, and it's a feeling I don't get too often. "Axel isn't going to hurt you."

"But if Alec doesn't call or won't cut a deal, then what?"

"We'll worry about that when the time comes."

"So, if he calls today, what am I supposed to say to him?"

"Axel will tell you. He just wants the name of the

buyer for the guns so he can cut a new deal. If he gets that, you'll be going home."

A silence spreads between us, and then she asks, "What if I don't want to go back to him?"

"What are you talking about, Tessa?"

"What if I want to stay with you?"

My heart beats wildly in my chest. "That's not an option," I mutter. "You'll go back to Alec, and I'll hit the road."

"And pretend I never existed?"

"Something like that." *If only it's going to be that easy.*

TESSA

We ride the rest of the way in silence. Why the fuck did I put myself out there like that? Of course, he was going to knock me back. I laugh to myself. He's not even nice to me. He locked me in a fucking shed. *I have the worst taste in men.*

The second Pit stops the bike, I climb off and hand the helmet back. "Look, Tessa," he begins, but I give an awkward smile and turn my back. The sooner we pretend that conversation didn't happen, the better.

I stare up at the large building. Axel heads over to us and whistles, then a man comes rushing over, looking eager to please. "Take Tessa down the basement," he says firmly.

My eyes widen and I look back at Pit, who is already protesting, but the man grabs my upper arm and begins to pull me away. "Please," I beg, "I won't misbehave."

"Pres, come on," snaps Pit, climbing off his bike. "You can put her in a room."

"She ain't a fucking guest," Axel replies. "Wasn't that what you kept telling me?"

"Pit," I cry desperately.

He watches, pained but rooted to the spot, while the man continues to drag me away. Suddenly, Pit breaks out into a run. "Let her go," he orders. The man looks past Pit to the President, who shakes his head, and he continues to drag me. Pit growls in frustration. "Now," he yells, and when the man stops again, Pit hits him in the face. I let out a surprised scream, and the man drops my arm and stumbles back. Pit pulls me to him.

"What the fuck was that?" demands Axel, marching towards us.

"She don't like the fucking dark," snaps Pit, keeping me to him. "She goes in a room or I take her back to the farm."

"That isn't your fucking call, Pit. She goes in the fucking basement."

Pit keeps me to him and begins to walk me away. "Please," I whisper, clinging to him.

"It's gonna be okay," he mutters.

"I can't go in there, Pit."

We go around the back of the building, and Pit pulls a metal door open. The sound of it scraping along the gravel rings out. I try to back away from him, but he holds me firm. "It's okay," he soothes. "I'll be with you."

I stare at the steps leading down into the basement and my chest tightens. "I can't breathe," I choke.

"I'm with you, Te. Every step." He lifts me, forcing me

to wrap my legs around his waist, and he carries me, leaving the door open. I squeeze my eyes closed and press my face into his neck, inhaling his spicy scent to distract me from the panic I currently feel.

"Don't leave me," I whisper.

We get to the bottom, and he steps into a large room with bars on the windows and the door. He doesn't bother to close them. Instead, he lowers to the ground, keeping me on his lap. "Never."

I glance around the room. It isn't as dark as I thought it would be, but come nightfall, I know I'm going to be terrified. "What is it about the dark?" he asks, gently moving hair from my face.

"When I was bullied," I blurt out without thinking. I've never told anyone the full story before.

"Keep going," he pushes.

"At secondary school. Steven Kendal. It was such a brutal time. It is for most kids, right? But he hated me from the second he laid eyes on me. He would do nasty things, like push me over every time he passed me or embarrass me in front of everyone by mocking me. He got all his friends to do the same, and then the girls would join in just to impress him. He was just cruel. And then, when we got to year eleven, he seemed to change his mind. Suddenly, he was nice and he'd go out his way to chat with me. I was wary at first, but after some time, I let my guard down."

"That doesn't explain why you hate the dark, Te."

I swallow the lump in my throat which appears whenever I think of Steven Kendal. I lower my eyes to the ground. "He asked me out on a date." Pit's eyes briefly close like he knows what's coming. "The first date was fine. He was charming and sweet. He said he'd been horrible because he really liked me but didn't think a pretty girl like me would give him the time of day. Anyway, I forgave him. The second date wasn't so good."

"Because?"

"He tried to kiss me, and I didn't let him. He got mad and tried to pin me down. Eventually, I let him kiss me because I got scared. He was so annoyed. Then he tried to . . . touch me, and I got upset, which only made him madder. He said he'd tell everyone what a frigid bitch I was unless I did stuff for him."

"Stuff?" repeats Pit, and I notice his jaw is clenched.

"Like oral sex and stuff," I mutter, lowering my eyes again.

"He forced himself on you?"

"I let him," I admit, "but I felt like I didn't have a choice." Tears fill my eyes. It's been so long since I thought about that time. "Date three, he tried it again, only this time, I refused."

"There was a date three?"

I shrug. "He turned up to my house without warning and basically ordered me to go with him. I was terrified he'd tell everyone about what we did."

"Jesus, Tessa."

"I stood up to him that night, and he didn't like it. He hit me . . . several times, in fact. And then he locked me in his shed until I agreed to do stuff again."

"And did you?"

"We began this warped relationship," I admit. "He'd be cruel, and I'd reward him." I swipe my tears from my cheeks. "It lasted a couple weeks before he got bored and moved on."

"So, he never . . ."

I shake my head. "We didn't have sex. Thankfully."

"Did you tell anyone?"

I shake my head again. "He said he'd tell everyone what I'd done and how I was scared of the dark." I scoff. "Funny enough, I don't think I was scared before he started locking me up."

"Jesus, Tessa," mutters Pit, pulling me to him. "I'm so sorry for all this shit."

"I just seem to fall for the wrong men." My words linger between us, but before he can respond, heavy footsteps descend the steps and Grizz appears in the doorway.

He stares for a moment, a slight smirk on his face. "Pres is calling church."

"Fill me in after," Pit mutters.

"I don't think that'll wash. Come tell him that yourself."

"If she's gotta stay down here, I'm staying too."

"Come on, Pit. Don't be an idiot."

"She's terrified of the dark," he spits angrily.

"It's not even dark," says Grizz, laughing.

"I'll be fine," I mutter, knowing full well I won't, but I don't want him to get into trouble.

"Is that stupid fucker coming or not?" yells Axel from the top of the steps.

"Doesn't look like it, Pres," Grizz answers.

"Jesus Christ, bring the girl," he bellows. "But you'll pay for it," he adds.

Pit gives me a satisfied smile and taps my thigh so I stand. He pushes to his feet and takes my hand in his.

We head back towards the building entrance, ducking under a half-open shutter which leads us into the huge room. There's a group of women sitting on two couches, all chatting, which stops when they notice me. Axel steps from a room. "In here," he barks, and I startle at his harsh tone.

We go inside the office, and I'm taken back to when they first brought me here. I was terrified back then and certain I was going to be killed. Now, I feel more at ease, even though Axel is glaring at me like I'm his biggest problem. He points to a chair, and I head in, sitting down. When I glance back, Pit is in the doorway. "Not you," snaps Axel, closing the door before he can protest. He locks it and then closes the blinds before rounding his desk. "Call him," he orders, sliding my phone to me. "He didn't reply to your little codeword text."

My hands shake as I pick up the phone. Without Pit here to save me, I'm nervous. I press call and then loudspeaker. It rings and goes to answer message. "Again," he snaps, so I press the call button again.

This time, it connects, and I sigh in relief. "Alec?" The line remains quiet. "Alec, can you hear me?"

"Where are you?" Hearing Alec's voice floods me with relief, and I almost sob out loud.

"Thank God."

"She's still alive," snaps Axel, "for now, but we really need to talk."

"I have fuck all to say to you," snaps Alec. "Tessa, where are you?"

"She ain't gonna tell you that while I have a gun to her head," snaps Axel, eyeing me in warning to keep up his lie, which I do without question because I have no idea if there's a weapon within his reach. "I want names of everyone involved in your little operation," he continues, "and I want the contact details of the people you sold my guns to."

"It ain't worth my life," he barks.

"And what about your wife's?" Axel asks.

"Tessa, I'm so sorry," he mutters.

My eyes widen. "Sorry?" I repeat. "What does that mean?"

"I can't help you."

"Are you fucking kidding?" I scream. "You're just leaving me here to die?"

"I don't even know you," he says, "not really."

"Well, fucking great, thanks a lot. I'm only in this mess because of you," I yell.

"Look, as much as I'm enjoying this lovers tiff, we need to come up with an arrangement, cos if we don't, you're gonna walk around with a price on your head," Axel interrupts.

"I can give you the name of my buyer," Alec eventually says, "but he won't deal with just anyone."

"He dealt with you, so I'm sure I can make him an offer he can't refuse."

"You want to cut a deal with him?"

"Well, my original deal fell through thanks to you, and now, I have a shit tonne of guns to get rid of before the police catch wind of them."

"Let me be your middleman. Keep me alive and I can

be useful for you," Alec offers. "I can get you a good deal."

Axel scoffs. "I can't trust you."

"What have you got to lose?" he asks. "We cut a deal and I can keep more coming your way."

"Keep talking."

"I deal with the Russians mainly, but I also have contacts in Ireland. If you can keep the supply coming, I can cut the deals."

I zone out, looking around the office and noticing a picture on the shelf of Axel on his bike with a woman behind him. She's one of the women who saw me come in here, but she didn't look the sort to hang around with a criminal gang.

Axel ends the call, bringing my attention back to him. "You might have luck on your side," he says, winking.

There's a knock on the door and he groans. "Go away."

"You'd better open this door right now," comes a female's voice, and he immediately goes to the door and unlocks it. The woman from the picture bursts in looking angry. "Why was the door locked? Why are the blinds down?" she demands.

I drop my eyes to the ground, cautious that she may go crazy thinking I was up to no good with her man. "Lexi, it's club business," Axel tells her calmly. "Relax." It was the wrong thing to say because he follows it with a quick apology, and I smirk to myself, realising he isn't in charge at all. Suddenly, he seems less scary.

"Relax?" she repeats, and I risk a quick glance up to see her hands on her hips and her eyes narrowed. "So, if I was to lock myself in your office with one of the guys, that would be okay?"

"Don't make me crazy," he growls, yanking her to him and pressing a kiss to her lips. "She's here until I can cut a deal."

She pulls free of his grasp, and he groans as she approaches me. I brace myself for a dressing-down, but she smiles and holds out her hand for me to shake, which I do. "I'm Lexi, this idiot's old lady."

"Lex," he mutters, his tone warning.

"I'm Tessa," I reply.

"Why do you look so terrified?" she asks, frowning. "Did someone hurt you?"

"Lexi," snaps Axel, more firmly this time.

"I just want to go home," I tell her.

"Enough," Axel barks, moving closer. Lexi puts up her hand, and he stops, placing his hands on his hips and staring down at the ground.

"From the beginning," she says to me.

"Pit took me from a warehouse and kept me at his farm." I rush the words before Axel can shut me down.

"It's not as simple as it sounds," Axel tries to explain.

She ignores him, so I continue. "And now, I'm here and staying in the basement."

Her eyes widen as she turns her angry expression to Axel. "Club business?" she repeats. "You're keeping this poor woman in the fucking basement?"

"And I'm scared of the dark," I whisper, almost smirking at Axel, who's glaring at me.

"Oh my god, did you know that when you put her in there?" she demands.

"Pit told him," I cut in.

"Have you lost your goddamn mind?" yells Lexi.

"Outside, now," orders Axel angrily. "Pit, come get this . . . this . . ." He shakes his head, lost for words. "Come get her out my office now," he finishes, and Pit appears holding ice to his jaw.

I rush to him. "What happened?"

"Nothing I can't handle," he says, glancing at Axel before taking my hand and leading me from the office.

"Church in five," Axel bellows after him before slamming the door.

"What was that all about?" Pit asks, taking me upstairs and into a bedroom.

"He made me call Alec. I think they've come to an arrangement."

"That's good," he says, sitting on the bed and pulling me beside him.

"And then Lexi came in wondering why the door was locked, and I told her that he's keeping me here against my will."

Pit winces but smirks. "I see that didn't go down well."

I shake my head and laugh. "Serves him right."

"Maybe you'll be back home before the day is through," Pit adds, and I note the sadness in his eyes.

"Maybe," I mutter.

"What's the plan with you two?" he asks.

I shrug. "I have no idea anymore. He was taking me on our honeymoon to consummate the marriage." Pit stares at the ground. "And he was going to buy us a new home when we returned."

"So, he's got money?" he asks, frowning.

I nod. "I think so."

"But you don't know?"

"He had nice pictures on his profile, a flashy car, and he got me a nice dress for the wedding."

"But you didn't see any cash beforehand?"

"He was transferring when we got married, but I never got the chance to check."

He gives a stiff nod. "Okay. Get some rest. It's been a crazy morning. I'll have to lock the door, but you understand, right?"

I nod, and he places a gentle kiss on my forehead. I close my eyes and savour the feel of his thumb brushing over my cheek. He stands, and I open my eyes to find him staring at me longingly. "What happened?" I ask again, nodding to the ice pack.

"I got off lightly for disrespecting my President."

"And that's the man you look up to?" I ask, arching a brow. "You need better friends."

He laughs as he heads for the door. "It's all good, Te."

CHAPTER 10

PIT

I get into church and drop down in my seat, ignoring the glares from Axel as he waits for the room to fill up. I'll apologise, but not in front of everyone.

He bangs the gavel on the table, and the brothers quiet down. "We've finally had contact with Alec Clay. He's offered us a deal."

"Is he in a position to cut a deal?" asks Fletch, laughing.

"Well, seems he doesn't really give a shit if he sees his virgin bride again," says Axel, and I finally meet his eyes. That fucker isn't fighting to get her back and that pisses me off. She deserves better.

"She's not part of the deal?" I ask, trying to stop the feeling of hope from building in my chest, because there can be none. I need to get back on the road.

"Oh, he's getting her back," says Axel firmly. "She's not our problem."

"She still saw what I did," I point out.

"And I don't think she'll be in a rush to report you, do you?" he asks, arching a brow.

I'm aware of the other brothers staring back and forth between us, wondering what all the tension is. "But just to cover your back, we have a solution," says Grizz, bringing my attention to him. "You'll take her on this job," he continues, sliding a piece of paper towards me with an address on it. I groan, knowing this isn't going to end well. "She's going to help you."

"No fucking way," I snap.

Axel stands, slamming his hands on the table. "We're trying to clean up this fucking mess," he bellows, "so you'll fucking work with us." I resist the urge to roll my eyes, staring hard at the paper until my vision blurs. He lowers back into his chair. "She can help clean up. That way, she's an accessory."

"Not if she goes to the police and tells them everything," I point out.

Coop nods in agreement. "He's right. If she tells the police she was terrified, they'll put her in witness protection."

"She's been fucking bullied most of her life," says Grizz, and I stare at him. He grins. "I overheard your little heart to heart."

Anger rushes through me and I stand, making a grab for him over the table. He leans back, narrowly escaping, and the brothers closest to me drag me back into my seat. "That's fucking sick," I yell, "using her vulnerability like that."

"What choice do you have?" yells Axel. "You wanna risk it?"

I take a calming breath, and my brothers release me, all going back to their seats. "You know you'll pay for that, right?" asks Grizz, smirking. He's going to kick my arse properly this time, and I won't have a choice but to take it.

"Let's focus on the task at hand," snaps Axel. "That fucker has contacts in Russia and Ireland."

"We can't trust him," says Fletch.

"Of course, we can't," says Axel, "but we lost our deal and it's taking time for them to get on board again. You know the Chinese hate being let down, and selling in London ain't making us enough. If we can get these contacts, we can end Alec further down the line."

"What's the deal?" asks Coop.

"A seventy-to-thirty split, but I've knocked him down to twenty percent until trust is established."

"And the woman?" asks Coop.

"She stays for now. When the deal goes through and money is finalised, she goes back to him."

My heart stutters, but I give an approving nod. If we do this deal, my life can go back to how it was. Just me, the road, and my dogs.

"It's the only choice we have right now," adds Grizz. "We have to move those guns and soon. We've had them sitting there for far too long."

"If everyone is happy," says Axel, glancing around the room, "then we can get on with our day. I'll let you know when a deal is struck." He bangs the gavel and everyone moves out, leaving me, Axel, and Grizz alone.

The second the door closes, Axel is out his chair. His fist connects with my chin in the exact same spot Grizz got me less than an hour ago, and I hiss as pain radiates through my skull. "You fucking disrespect me again, I'll take your eyes out," he yells, adding a punch to my gut. I drop from my chair to my knees, coughing, and he storms from the room.

Grizz looms over me, and I brace myself for his onslaught, but instead, he holds out his hand for me to take. I grab it warily, and he helps me to my feet, patting me on the back extra hard. "I figure you're in enough pain," he says, smirking. "It's gonna get a whole lot worse once you let her go."

I frown. "Huh?"

"Tessa," he says. "You've fallen for her."

"Bullshit," I mutter, rubbing my jaw.

"I heard the way you were, brother. Axel sees it too. That's why he got her back here. Leaving you two alone would be a disaster. There's only so long you can restrain yourself, right?" He laughs. "I'm impressed you've gone this long."

"Usually, I just pull the trigger," I mutter, following him from the room. "I don't get to know them."

"And that's where you went wrong," he replies. "Just do this job tonight and then avoid her, man. She's married, and part of the deal will be getting her back to her husband in one piece and intact." He slaps me on the back again before heading for Axel's office.

I go out to my bike. I need to feel the rush of speed and forget about this shit for now.

TESSA

There's a light knock on the bedroom door before a

key turns and it opens. Lexi sticks her head in, smiling, "Hi. Are you okay?"

I give a nod, and she steps inside, closing the door behind her. "Axel said I could bring you some food," she adds, holding out a plate for me, and I take it. "I hope cheese sandwiches are okay."

I nod, picking one up and taking a bite. "I love cheese."

"I think you'll be going home soon enough," she adds, and I stare as she takes a seat beside me. "I overheard them talking about it." I give a slight nod and place the sandwich back on the plate. I don't know why I'm suddenly filled with dread. "You don't look so happy," she pushes.

I sigh. "I don't really have a home. Well, not yet."

"They mentioned your husband?"

"I've only just married him. It's his fault I'm here." I give an empty laugh. "I had it all figured out, and now, this has happened and it's made me think it all over. What if I've made a mistake?"

She smiles kindly, placing her hand over mine. "You can always leave your marriage."

"I guess."

"Unless . . . well, unless you're scared of your husband?"

I shrug. "I don't know him."

Lexi frowns. "How come?"

"It was more of a business deal than a marriage," I admit. "And now, my eyes have been opened," I add.

She gives a knowing smile. "Pit?"

"He's not as bad as I thought."

"They never are," she says with a laugh. "Have you told him?"

I nod. "He's not interested. At least, that's what he says."

"Yah know, it could just be that you've been with him too long and you're reading into things too much. Go home and then see how you feel."

The door opens and Pit comes in. I'm instantly relieved. He's been gone most of the day, and I was starting to worry that Axel had sent him home. Lexi stands. "I'll come back tomorrow to check on you," she offers, and I nod in agreement.

Pit doesn't meet my eyes, but he hands me a set of clothes in black. "Get changed."

I stare at the leggings and hoodie. "Are we going somewhere?"

"I have a job to get to, and you're coming."

"I am?" I'm surprised, seeing as earlier they didn't trust me to even leave the door unlocked. "How come?"

"Tessa," he mutters, taking my chin between his thumb and fingers, "don't ask me questions. Just trust me and it'll all be over soon." He presses his lips to mine and then steps back, immediately leaving me cold. He tugs his hood up, something I haven't seen him do in weeks, and then he sits on the edge of the bed, staring at the floor, waiting for me to change.

∽

WE RIDE for twenty minutes before he stops the bike outside a bungalow. It's quiet, with dim streetlights and no traffic around. The only other building nearby is a school, which is obviously closed. I get off the bike. "Keep your helmet on," says Pit, also climbing off. "And whatever you do, don't make a noise."

"What's happening?" I ask as he takes my hand and leads me towards the bungalow.

"Remember what I said," he adds.

He tries the door, and it opens. "Aren't you going to knock?" I whisper. He gently squeezes my hand, reminding me to be quiet.

We go inside, and Pit heads straight for a door at the end of the hallway. He twists the knob and shoves it, releasing my hand as he steps inside. An elderly man sits in an armchair. He doesn't look at all surprised to see us. "Finally," he says, smiling.

"That's all you got to say?" asks Pit, taking off his helmet. I go to do the same, but Pit stops me, shaking his head.

"I've been waiting for weeks," the man replies. "You took your time."

"See, I'd be begging right about now," snaps Pit.

"Why would I?" asks the man. "It won't help. I'll save it for when the devil gets hold of me."

"Scum," Pit mutters, taking out a knife from his back pocket. He removes the leather sheath, and I stare wide-eyed as I back away a few steps.

"I don't regret anything," the man spits, suddenly sounding angry. "It's natural. In some countries, it's legal."

"Then you should have moved," snaps Pit, gripping the man by the collar. He doesn't fight, and I stare, mesmerised at how calm he looks considering his situation.

"You shouldn't judge me, biker, until you've felt the buzz of that tight little pussy—" Pit slices the knife across the man's cheek, carving a line from one ear to the other. I back away a few more steps until I hit the wall. My chest tightens, and as blood pours down the man's chin, I grip my stomach, praying I don't vomit into the helmet.

"I *am* judging you," sneers Pit, and I see the man I first met, that cold and angry biker. "And when I get to hell, I'll make your life misery." He pushes the knife between the man's legs, and he gurgles in pain, his eyes rolling back into his head. Pit twists the knife, causing the man to jerk before he passes out. I watch in horror as Pit drags the blade from the man's groin, up through his stomach, only stopping when the blade snags on something. Then he pulls it free and slices the man's throat.

I rush out the room, pulling at my helmet and throwing it to the floor before dropping down beside it and vomiting onto the dirty carpet. I squeeze my eyes closed, picturing the blood spilling from the man and onto the floor. More vomit leaves me, and I sit back on my feet, wiping my mouth across my sleeve.

I feel Pit's presence behind me. "He deserved it," he mutters.

Rage replaces the sickness as I push to my feet, shoving him hard in the chest. "You fucking bastard," I scream.

"Remember what I said," he hisses. "You have to be quiet."

"In case I wake the fucking dead?" I yell, shoving him

again. He doesn't budge, which frustrates me more. "Why did you bring me here?"

"Two reasons," he says, not quite meeting my eyes. "The first, so you see who I really am. The second, because I'm following orders."

"This is not who you are," I cry. "You're pushing me away because of what I said." Tears begin to fall, and I swipe at them angrily. "I get it, you don't want me, but you don't have to make me watch this bullshit."

He finally meets my eyes and that haze he had there while he sliced into that man is lifted, replaced with what I think is guilt. "You were sick," he mutters, nodding to the stained carpet behind me. "Evidence you were here."

I inhale sharply. "Fuck."

"We need to leave."

"Leave?" I repeat, panic setting in once again. "But I need to clean that up. If we use bleach or . . ." I flap my hands in panic, looking around me. "Maybe he has some," I add, rushing for the nearest door and shoving it open. It's the bathroom, and I go in, pulling open the cupboard and dragging the contents out onto the floor. "Shit, there's nothing." I glance back to find Pit leaning in the doorway, watching me. I can't place the look on his face, but I know I don't like it. I stand, turning to him. "Why aren't you helping me?"

"This is my insurance," he mutters. The ringing in my ears dials up a notch until it's the only sound I hear over the thumping of my heart. "If you go to the police about anything, I'll tie you into this murder."

"But I . . . I didn't . . ." My words trail off. The

betrayal burns me so deep, it's hard to breathe let alone say the words rushing through my mind.

"You were in the room while a man died and you did nothing, Tessa. You're an accessory, and if I get caught for any of it, I'm taking you down with me."

"But if they find my DNA here," I whisper, the words sounding broken through my heavy breaths, "they'll arrest me anyway."

"Cleaners are on their way. But I have your pictures." He holds out his mobile, and I stare at the image of me vomiting on the carpet.

"That doesn't show murder," I spit. "It shows me reacting to something I didn't like."

"Are you willing to take the risk, Te?" I'd fallen in love with the way he'd shortened my name, but right now, it makes my skin crawl. "I just need one more picture," he adds, and the words feel like he's forcing them out. He reaches for me, but I step back, almost slipping on the bathroom floor. He grabs me, yanking me from the room and shoving me into the living room. I freeze, staring at the man bleeding out as his dead eyes stare blankly at me. A sob escapes me, and I slam my hands over my mouth. The flash of a camera makes me look back to where Pit is snapping photos of me next to the body.

"No," I scream, rushing at him but slipping and losing my footing. My hands save me as I crash to the ground, but I realise too late they're in the blood and I slide, landing on my stomach. I lift my hand and stare at the sticky fluid. "Oh god," I whisper. Then I scramble back, trying to stand but only covering myself further. "Shit," I hiss.

Hands reach under my arms and I'm hauled to my feet. "We need to go," he whispers, startling me.

He leads me towards the door, pushing my helmet onto my head as he opens it. I begin to wipe my hands down my leggings, discovering those are soaked in blood too, smearing it further up my arms. I sob silently as I climb on the bike. Instead of holding on to Pit, I grip the bar behind me. I don't want any contact with him whatsoever. I hate him.

CHAPTER 11

PIT

She does everything she can to stop her body touching any part of me. Even as we round bends, she fights the natural law of gravity, keeping her thighs from clenching around me. Robert Woods was a paedophile, but he was also a well-respected man in his community. A school caretaker who managed to secure a place on the governor's board, embedding himself deeper into the heart of his very own playground. He ran workshops for the kids who struggled to learn. He offered fishing trips to kids who couldn't control their behaviour or temper, telling them it was therapeutic.

His sick games only came to light a week ago, when the headteacher's grandson, now twenty-six years old, came forward and exposed everything. It was embarrassing for the school and more so for the governors. We were paid a lot of money to make the problem go away as quietly as possible. But I can't tell Tessa any of that. I needed that evidence as much as I need to let her go. Axel is right, I can't risk her rushing to the police the second she gets her freedom back. And at least this way, she keeps her life.

She jumps from the bike the second we get back and removes her helmet, shoving it against my chest. Then I watch as she rounds the back of the building. I get off the bike just as Axel comes out. "Done?" he asks.

"Yep," I mutter, pulling out my mobile to send him the photographs.

"Where'd she go?" he asks, nodding in the direction Tessa ran off.

"I dunno, to clear her head, I think." She won't get far, so I don't rush after her, but once Axel is back inside, I head off in that direction. I stop by the open basement door. There's no way she'd be down there alone. No way. But as I stare out across the dark field, I can't make out any movement.

"Te?" I call out. There's no reply, so I head down the stone steps. I find her sitting on the floor with her knees pulled up to her chest and her forehead resting on them. "Te?" I repeat, but she doesn't respond. "You hate it down here. Come inside."

"Go away," she mutters, and I realise she's crying.

"You'd rather stay here in the dark, alone, than come inside and shower?" I ask.

"Yes."

"He deserved it," I tell her again.

"I didn't," she mutters. Then she looks up and the moonlight catches the angry look in her eyes. "I didn't deserve any of this." She throws her bloodied arms up in the air in exasperation. "I just wanted to get married and have some fucking stability in my crappy life. For once, I wanted to be happy," she cries. "And somehow, I ended up here, meeting you," she spits the words like they leave a bad taste in her mouth. "And now, my life is more fucked-up than it's ever been."

"Tessa," I mutter, unable to find the words she needs to feel better about any of this. I sigh heavily. "It was just crap timing. Wrong place and wrong time."

"That's it?" she yells, pushing to her feet. "That's all you have to explain the shitty way you've treated me and continue to treat me?"

"What did you expect?" I yell, and she takes a step back. "You sold yourself to a scumbag. That was never gonna end well. What kind of man buys a virgin? What sort of morals is he going to have, Tessa?"

"You just killed a man in cold blood," she screams angrily. "Don't speak to me about morals."

"I have morals," I hiss through gritted teeth. "If I didn't, I'd have fucked you by now."

She scoffs. "I'm so fucking happy you didn't."

"Bullshit," I spit. "You've been desperate for me since you started sucking my cock."

"You make me sick."

"I make you horny, and you fucking hate it. Your body reacts to me, and you lose control," I say, smirking. "If I pushed you against that wall right now," I add, stepping closer, "and kissed you . . ." I back her to the wall without touching her, and she inhales sharply, tipping her head back to look at me with disdain. "You'd let me. Do you know why?" She gives her head a slight shake. "Because you want me." I press my lips to hers, swiping my tongue gets her freedom back. And at least this way, she keeps her life.

She jumps from the bike the second we get back and removes her helmet, shoving it against my chest. Then I watch as she rounds the back of the building. I get off the bike just as Axel comes out. "Done?" he asks.

"Yep," I mutter, pulling out my mobile to send him the photographs.

"Where'd she go?" he asks, nodding in the direction Tessa ran off.

"I dunno, to clear her head, I think." She won't get far, so I don't rush after her, but once Axel is back inside, I head off in that direction. I stop by the open basement door. There's no way she'd be down there alone. No way. But as I stare out across the dark field, I can't make out any movement.

"Te?" I call out. There's no reply, so I head down the stone steps. I find her sitting on the floor with her knees pulled up to her chest and her forehead resting on them. "Te?" I repeat, but she doesn't respond. "You hate it down here. Come inside."

"Go away," she mutters, and I realise she's crying.

"You'd rather stay here in the dark, alone, than come inside and shower?" I ask.

"Yes."

"He deserved it," I tell her again.

"I didn't," she mutters. Then she looks up and the moonlight catches the angry look in her eyes. "I didn't deserve any of this." She throws her bloodied arms up in the air in exasperation. "I just wanted to get married and have some fucking stability in my crappy life. For once, I wanted to be happy," she cries. "And somehow, I ended up here, meeting you," she spits the words like they leave a bad taste in her mouth. "And now, my life is more fucked-up than it's ever been."

"Tessa," I mutter, unable to find the words she needs to feel better about any of this. I sigh heavily. "It was just crap timing. Wrong place and wrong time."

"That's it?" she yells, pushing to her feet. "That's all you have to explain the shitty way you've treated me and continue to treat me?"

"What did you expect?" I yell, and she takes a step back. "You sold yourself to a scumbag. That was never gonna end well. What kind of man buys a virgin? What sort of morals is he going to have, Tessa?"

"You just killed a man in cold blood," she screams angrily. "Don't speak to me about morals."

"I have morals," I hiss through gritted teeth. "If I didn't, I'd have fucked you by now."

She scoffs. "I'm so fucking happy you didn't."

"Bullshit," I spit. "You've been desperate for me since you started sucking my cock."

"You make me sick."

"I make you horny, and you fucking hate it. Your body reacts to me, and you lose control," I say, smirking. "If I pushed you against that wall right now," I add, stepping closer, "and kissed you . . ." I back her to the wall without touching her, and she inhales sharply, tipping her head back to look at me with disdain. "You'd let me. Do you know why?" She gives her head a slight shake. "Because you want me." I press my lips to hers, swiping my tongue against hers and placing my hands against the wall either side of her head.

Her fists come between us, shoving hard at my chest. I laugh, breaking the kiss and stumbling back. "Get out," she growls, wiping her mouth on the back of her hand. "And don't come back."

I snigger, trying to hide my anger. "Fine, Te. Enjoy it down here covered in another man's blood."

By the time I get into the clubhouse, I'm raging. I almost turned back more than once to drag her back here, but walking away is a good thing. It's the break I need to stop this bullshit idea I have in my head that we can be something more.

Axel is at the bar nursing a whiskey. I head over and take the seat beside him. He glances behind me and asks, "Where is she?"

"Basement."

He smirks. "Thought she hated the dark."

"She does."

"Right." He frowns but chooses not to comment further. Instead, he nods to the prospect, who pours me a drink before topping up Axel's glass. "You've got your evidence. That will protect you. I'll make the arrangements for her to go back where she belongs."

"Okay," I mutter, knocking my drink back.

"And you can hit the road when you're ready."

"Right."

"Are you ready?" he asks, side-eyeing me.

The prospect tops me up again. "Yep."

"Cos if you're not, brother, and you wanna stick around . . ."

"Why would I wanna stick around?" I ask, knocking back the second.

"Maybe it's just time," he says with a shrug.

"For what?"

He smirks again. "Yah know, settling down, finding someone."

"It's not for me."

He openly laughs, and I glare at him. "I saw the way you were with her, Pit. I saw the same in myself, and then in Grizz, and even with Fletch. All of us swore we didn't want a woman, until we met the one, and now look at us."

"Yeah, well, I'm not like you. I like my solo life, and I like the road."

"Okay, well, I'll have her moved out ASAP." He pushes to stand. "Then you can get back to normal. We all can."

He walks away, and I stare into my empty glass. *Fuck her.* She isn't my problem. I turn the glass a few times. She was never even mine to begin with.

I growl and push to my feet, stalking out the clubhouse and rounding the back again. I sit on the top step of the basement and listen to her sobs. *Fuck.*

"I'm sorry," I say, and her sobbing quiets. "I didn't mean for any of it. I was just doing the same shit I've always done. It was just another job, and then you came along and . . ." I place my head in my hands and groan. "You turned my life upside down." She sniffles quietly, and my heart cracks. "I needed insurance because I can't risk going to prison. And deep down, I know you're not gonna rat me out, but Axel wasn't happy with your word.

He was looking out for me." She doesn't reply, so I sigh, "Please come and shower, Te. Please."

I hear a shuffling sound, and then her hands wrap around the bars at the bottom gate. I smile to myself and head down to unlock it. She keeps her eyes to the ground but allows me to take her by the hand and lead her up the steps and back to the clubhouse.

TESSA

I'm shaking uncontrollably, and I don't know if I'm in shock, cold, or just terrified from being alone in that damn basement.

Pit takes me to his bedroom, where he leaves me standing in the middle of the room while he goes into his en-suite. I hear the shower turn on and raise my eyes to catch a glimpse of myself in the mirror. I'm smeared in blood. It's dried on, making my skin feel tight. Pit comes back in and stops, looking unsure as I stare wide-eyed at my reflection. Eventually, he takes my top and begins to carefully pull it over my head. Then he kneels before me and taps my foot, so I lift it, and he removes my trainers. He hooks his fingers in my leggings and peels them down my legs. More dried blood is revealed, and a sob escapes me.

Pit removes my underwear and quickly leads me to the bathroom, which is now full of steam. "I'll wait outside," he mutters as I step into the shower and stand under the spray, closing my eyes. When I don't reply, he sighs heavily. "Te, you gotta scrub yourself." But I don't want to touch the blood, not now it's wet again and running down my body.

A minute later, he steps into the cubicle naked. *He's naked.* He doesn't meet my eyes as he grabs the sponge and covers it in his shower gel. He lifts my arm out and begins to scrub my skin. I watch the water turning red as it drains away. He does the same to my other arm then crouches before me and begins rubbing the sponge down each leg, careful not to touch me anywhere else.

When he stands again, his cock is hard. He rinses the sponge and throws it out the cubicle and into the bin. Then he takes his shampoo and squirts it onto my hair. He stands closer, his erection brushing my stomach as he works his fingers into my scalp, lathering the shampoo. He gently tugs my hair so my head goes right back, and then he begins to rinse. Now, all I can think about is his cock and how each time he moves, it prods me. I clench my teeth in frustration. It doesn't matter what he does, somehow, I always end up wanting him anyway. He's right. Everything he said is right. *I can't fucking resist him.* And I hate that.

When he's satisfied my hair is clean, he gives a slight smile. "That's better. All clean."

I bite on my lower lip, stopping myself from saying anything because I don't trust myself. His eyes fix there and he places his thumb just below it, gently tugging it free. "You're making this too hard," he whispers.

My hands glide over his chest, and I feel his heart hammering wildly. I run them up and over his shoulders, cupping the back of his neck and standing on my tiptoes as I bring his lips closer. His eyes burn into mine as I swipe my tongue over his lower lip. He opens slightly, and I kiss him. He keeps his hands by his sides, letting me know this is at my pace, and as I run my hand down to his shaft, gripping it tightly like he's shown me, he hisses, closing his eyes. I smile to myself. I love seeing him come apart, but right now, all I want is to feel him inside me.

I move my hand a few times, feeling his cock swell. The kiss becomes hungrier as I reach behind us to turn the shower off. He takes the hint and picks me up, wrapping my legs around his waist. His erection is right at my opening, but no amount of wiggling makes him fuck me. I've tried it too many times.

He takes us to the bed. Not bothering to grab a towel, he lays me down, kissing down my neck and along my collar bone. "I want us to . . ." I begin, and he pauses, glancing up to meet my eyes. "Please," I whisper, feeling my face burn with embarrassment.

"You know we can't," he mutters.

"But I want to."

"You're married."

"I don't want to think about any of that," I tell him.

"Axel is sending you—"

"Please," I say firmly, cutting off his words. "For one night, I want to be normal."

He drops down beside me and lays his arm over his eyes. "You're making this impossible," he mutters.

I see my opportunity and climb over him. He removes his arm and his eyes shoot open, but I've already lined his cock at my entrance. "Te," he shouts out as I sink down onto him.

Pain rips through me, and I cry out, digging my nails into his chest and squeezing my eyes closed. I'm frozen, too scared to move in case the burning pain rips through me again. As it subsides, I relax slightly, risking a look at Pit. He's staring wide-eyed. "It's done now," I mutter, feeling stupid.

"Get off," he says quietly.

I swallow hard, placing my hands flat on his chest and slowly pushing myself up. The pain isn't as bad, but I wince as it stings. Sitting beside him, I stare at the floor and wait for his rejection. Instead, his fingers gently run down my spine. "That's not how your first time should be," he mutters.

"It's what I want."

"Is it?" he asks, sitting up. "Earlier, you said you hated me."

"It's like a compulsion," I mutter. "I hate you, but I can't stop wanting you."

"It's not real," he says. "You said it yourself—you're not here because you want to be."

"If you left the door wide open right now," I say, glancing at him, "I wouldn't leave."

"It's not locked," he points out.

"And I'm still here."

"Then go, Te. Let me go to sleep, and then run out of here."

"And go where?" I cry, standing. I glance down at the blood on his semi-erect shaft and gasp. "Oh god, did I do that?" I look down between my legs and see smeared blood between my thighs. I instantly panic, holding my hands over my mouth as my breathing comes in rapid bursts.

Pit stands, gripping my wrists and crouching slightly to

look me in the eye. "Te, I'm not hurt. Neither of us are. That happens on the first time."

"I know that," I cry, "but there's so much."

He smiles, pulling me to him and wrapping his arms around me. "It's normal."

I look up, and he's staring down at me, still smiling. "We need clothes," he mutters, his smile fading. His laboured breathing matches mine, and his eyes darken. "Before we do something we regret." And then he slams his mouth against mine, kissing me hungrily. I daren't move or speak in case I spook him, so I allow his hands to roam my body as he claims my mouth.

He guides me backwards until my legs hit against the bed, and then we lower, me on my back and him braced over me. My legs fall open, and his cock rubs against me. I cup his face, grazing my nails over his neck and down his back. He breaks the kiss and rests his forehead against mine, peering down between us. "Fuck it," he mutters, almost to himself.

I feel pressure as he presses the head of his cock to my opening, and in one swift move, he's inside me, filling me up again. I close my eyes, gasping in surprise. "Relax," he whispers, pressing a kiss to my forehead. I try, taking a deep breath and releasing it slowly. "I'm going to move," he tells me. "I promise it gets better." I give a stiff nod, and he smiles.

Placing a hand under my neck and using the other to tease my nipple, he begins to slide from me. He takes his time, gauging my reaction, and with each wince, he pauses, waiting for me to relax again before moving.

He lowers his mouth to my erect nipple and takes it in,

swirling his tongue around it. I relax some more, enjoying the way he teases me. When he slides back inside me, it's not so sore.

After a few more times, he groans, resting his forehead against mine again. "I'm gonna pull out and put a condom on. I need to be inside you when I come."

He leans over to the bedside cabinet and retrieves a condom, kneeling up and ripping it open. I watch as he sheathes his erection, ignoring the blood.

When he settles back between my legs, he takes each of my hands and pins them beside my head, lacing our fingers together. "You good?" he asks, staring at me intently.

"Yes," I whisper.

He smiles. "I'm sorry for what's about to happen."

I frown, but before I can ask, he pushes into me, and I cry out. This time, he doesn't take his time. He slams into me and withdraws equally as quick, repeating it over and over. At first, it's uncomfortable, but the faster he moves, the nicer it feels, like a scratch finally being itched.

He's panting hard, and when he releases my hand, he grabs the back of my knee and lifts my leg, pushing it towards my chest. This time, when he sinks into me, I feel him on a whole new level.

I watch his expressions. He's completely lost, fucking me like he's on a mission, like he can no longer see me. And then he growls. It's deep, coming from the back of his throat. He stills, occasionally jerking but keeping his eyes closed as he enjoys his orgasm.

After a few minutes of silence, his heavy breaths slowing, he withdraws and heads for the bathroom. He returns minus the bloody condom and holding a washcloth. "Are you okay?" he asks.

I nod. He sits at the end of the bed and parts my legs, forcing them apart when I try to resist. He gently wipes me clean, folding the cloth a few times before throwing it in the corner of the room. "It gets better," he repeats. "The first time is always terrible."

I feel my cheeks redden. "Was I terrible?"

His smile fades and he realises he's offended me. "Shit, no, Te. You were fucking amazing. I meant, it's not as good for you because it's your first time. For me, it was . . . fucking mind- blowing."

I relax slightly, watching as he goes to his drawers and pulls out a T-shirt, handing it to me to put on.

Then he slides into bed, pulling the sheets back for me to slip under. "We need a plan," he mutters, pulling me into his arms and wrapping himself around me like vines. The T-shirt rides up and I feel his cock pressed against my backside.

"A plan?" I ask.

"To keep you here," he mumbles sleepily. "Forever."

～

I LIE AWAKE, staring at the ceiling and thinking over his words. *Forever. Keep me here forever.* A stray tear slides down my cheek. Forever with Pit. *Forever.* I wipe my wet cheeks, slipping one leg from underneath him. Whenever we share a bed, he sleeps with me glued to him, his arms encasing me, his legs over my own. It makes me feel safe, but right now, I feel claustrophobic. He's a murderer. He kills in cold blood and smiles while he does it. He's held me here for weeks and forced me into a situation that means he'll always have something to hold over me. Forever can't be with him.

I get my leg free and work on the other, carefully pulling it from under his body. His arms tighten, and he stirs. I freeze, holding my breath as his hand finds my breast, cupping it and gently teasing the nipple. Even in his sleep, he's thinking about sex.

I wait for him to settle before trying again, carefully taking his arm and placing a pillow there instead. He immediately grabs onto it, tucking it into his arms. I smile, taking one last look at his face before sliding from the bed and going to the bathroom.

I pace. *Shit. Shit. Shit.* Now what?

I dress quickly in a discarded pair of shorts from Pit, tucking in the T-shirt to hold them up. I pick up my trainers, carrying them so I don't wake him with my footsteps.

I creep back through the bedroom, holding my breath as I ease the door open, pulling it slowly. I glance back to see Pit still blissfully unaware as I slip from the room and rush along the landing. At the top of the stairs, I push my feet into my trainers and run down, coming to an abrupt stop when Axel steps from his office. It's the early hours of the morning, what the fuck is he doing awake?

He takes in my trainers and brings his eyes to meet mine. "In here," he orders.

I curse under my breath but follow him into his office. "I can only assume you and Pit have fucked up my deal?"

I don't bother to answer, staring hard at the floor

instead. "I'm gonna call your husband and tell him you're ready to leave."

My chest tightens, but I give a stiff nod. "And you're gonna keep your secrets, yours and Pit's, because the alternative is non-negotiable. My reach is deep, Tessa. The second you enter a police station, I'll know. Are we understanding one another?" I nod again. "Words," he yells, and I jump in fright.

"Yes."

"Your husband can't know what you and Pit have done. He paid for a virgin and that is what you are."

"Yes."

He picks up his phone and sends off a text. "Does Pit know you've left?" I shake my head. Humiliation grips me. "Good. I'll tell him you asked to go home." I finally look him in the eye. "What? You'd rather he thinks you snuck out of here with no money, no phone, and no clue where to go? Wasn't that the plan?" He laughs. "Jesus, how long did you think you'd last out there on the streets?"

"I didn't want to hurt him," I mutter.

He scoffs. "Pit? You think his heart is beating? You're naïve, Tessa. If you take anything away from all this, it should be not to trust anyone. Whatever you think Pit felt for you is bullshit. He was doing a job. Acting is all part of it. But I'm glad to know he's doing it well." His phone beeps and he glances at it. "He's on his way. He wants you to wait outside at the gates."

CHAPTER 12

PIT

I wake with a start and sit up, looking around. Something feels off, and when I glance beside me to see Tessa gone, that sinking feeling only worsens. "Te?" I call out, hoping she's in the bathroom but already knowing she isn't. I sigh heavily.

I dress and head downstairs. Maybe she just went for breakfast. I almost laugh at myself trying to reason with my heart to stop it from breaking. *Breaking?* What the fuck? See, this is the reason I should have kept my distance. I shake my head angrily as I burst into the kitchen.

The table is lined with hungry brothers who all turn to me when the door smacks back against the wall. Axel arches a brow, but something about his smug smile makes me zone in on him. "Where is she?"

"Brother, you already know."

"No," I yell, balling my fists at my sides.

"She came to me, Pit," he says, standing. "She asked

me to send her home. And we'd already agreed on that, right?"

My chest aches and my heart twists painfully. "No," I repeat, shaking my head.

"You knew we had to hand her back," he says calmly.

Fletch heads towards me. "Come on, brother, let's go somewhere else before you get another beating." He tries to put his hand on my shoulder, but I shrug him off angrily, spinning on my heel and heading out the kitchen.

"Don't take him to my office," Axel calls out. "I don't need him breaking shit."

"Jesus, Axel, what's gotten into you?" yells Lexi, and I hear her footsteps running up behind me.

"Pit," she calls, "wait." I push out into the fresh air, inhaling deeply. Fletch appears in my side vision, standing cautiously to my left. Lexi runs in front, spinning to face me and walking backwards.

"You know he's right," says Fletch. "She had to go back."

"I don't think she'll go to the police, Pit," adds Lexi, and I laugh coldly. Trust her to think that's what's upsetting me.

"She can't. We saw to that," I spit angrily.

"You're upset she's gone?" she asks, her voice laced with sadness. "Oh, Pit."

"I don't need your pity," I snap, storming off around the side of the building. I run down the steps and into the empty basement. Maybe a small part of me hoped she'd be hiding here, but when I see she's not here either, I crouch down and hang my head, allowing the pain to freeze my heart.

Lexi's footfalls descend the stairs, and I feel her presence in the doorway. "I hate it down here," she mutters, remaining by the door.

I drop back onto my arse and rest my arms on my raised knees. "It's not meant to be inviting," I say. "You shouldn't be down here anyway, especially not alone without your old man."

She rolls her eyes. "The rules are stupid."

I snigger. "Tell him that to his face."

"Why did she have to go back?" she asks.

"Club business," I mutter.

"She really liked you."

I shake my head, staring at the dirty floor and wondering how many people we've left down here to bleed out. "It was all an act."

"It wasn't."

"She lured me in so I'd let my guard down and she could run."

"But she didn't run, did she? She asked Axel if she could go, and by the sounds of things, you'd already agreed to it."

"Doesn't make it . . ." I pause, feeling like a pussy for even thinking the words.

"Hurt any less," she finishes for me. "So, go and tell her how you feel."

"He can't," comes Axel's voice, and she turns to look up the steps. "We made a deal with her husband, and The Chaos Demons don't break deals."

"Even for a brother?" she demands.

"Don't question what you don't understand, Lex," he warns, coming down the steps and joining her in the doorway.

"You said you'd do anything for your men," she argues. "Even die for them. And here you are, letting Pit break because the woman he loves has left."

"I'm fine," I mutter.

"Pit knows the score," says Axel. "Leave us," he adds, and she sighs heavily.

"I'm around if you need anything," she tells me, and I notice Axel give her a warning glare before she rushes off up the steps.

Axel steps inside, kicking the dirt with his boot. "You know I had no choice."

"I know," I agree. "The club comes first."

"And she was ready to leave."

"Did she say anything?" I ask, finally bringing my eyes to his. He gives his head a shake, and I force a smile. "Great, well, back to business then."

"I know the road is calling, brother, but I could do with the manpower here until things settle." I inwardly groan. "I've called the prospect. He's gonna bring King and Gigi here. I need you at the club."

"Okay," I say, standing. "Did Alec say anything last night?"

"Just that he'd be in touch today."

~

DRINK NUMBS THE ACHE. As I knock back my fourth and it warms my insides, I smile, letting my head fall back on the couch. King hasn't stopped whining since he got here, and I can't help but think he's also pining for Tessa. My mind wanders back to her and what she's doing right now. She's probably laughing at me, telling her fuckwit husband how she blinded me with her pussy. If I hadn't seen the evidence for myself, I'd have questioned if she even was a virgin. *But, fuck, it felt so right.* I groan, and Gigi immediately sits up to look around.

"Don't those things ever relax?" asks London, sitting on the arm of the couch.

"They're looking out for me."

"Well, I'm hardly a threat, am I?" she asks, smiling. "You look lost, Pit."

"I'm all good."

"You sure? I could spend some time with you . . . alone."

"Nah," I mutter. Cos as much as fucking London might distract me right now, I know deep down I'll regret it.

Axel bellows from his office. "Church." I push to stand, leaving my empty glass on the table.

"Another time," I tell her, thankful for the escape.

Axel eyes me warily when I flop into my seat while the other brothers file into church. "Are you drunk?"

"Nope," I mutter.

He slides a bottle of water to me. "Well, sober the fuck up, we have a meet with Alec."

I sit up straighter, opening the bottle and gulping the water. Once everyone settles, he tells the brothers the same.

"He's bringing Pavel Oleg, a big player in the Russian Mafia."

"You have a name," I say, "so cut Alec out."

"It's not that simple," he says, irritated by my interruption. "Alec will send me a location, and once we set off, he's going to send a second one. He's not stupid. We've got to leave the kuttes behind, and I can only take two men."

I hold my breath, relieved when he says my name, followed by Grizz. "Once we get to the location, we'll have our phones removed. We'll be checked for wires."

"What the fuck?" snaps Coop. "Who's this guy think he is?"

"Right now, he's in charge," says Axel. "We have to cut him in on this deal before I can gain the trust of the others involved."

"So, we're licking this dick's arse?" I demand.

"Yep," says Grizz. "Unless you think you're not up to the role?"

I want to see this prick in the ground more than anyone, so I relax back in my chair and keep my mouth shut.

∼

WE SET off in the car after receiving strict instructions to leave the bikes and kuttes behind, and we're all dressed in black suits.

Axel stops the car at a set of gates and presses the buzzer. The gates draw open, and he drives along the gravel road until a large house comes into view. "What the fuck is this prick playing at?" mutters Grizz, looking out the window as we pull to a stop.

A valet comes over, taking the keys from Axel as we

get out. "I think we're about to find out," Axel replies as we head up the steps.

The door opens and a butler nods in greeting as we go inside. The place is heaving with people dressed up and drinking Champagne. "I feel so out of place," I complain as we move through to a main room.

"It's all a game to him. We can't kill him in a room full of people," says Axel.

"Watch me," I mutter, and he smirks.

A man comes over, and I instantly freeze. With her arm neatly tucked in his, Tessa stares at me, expressionless, like she doesn't know me.

TESSA

I have spent the entire day being scrubbed, prodded, and poked, and then forced into this overly tight dress which digs into my hips. My hair has so many pins holding it in place, I have no idea how the hell I'll ever find them all. And all I really want to do is sleep. My heart is heavy, and my eyes sting with unshed tears.

Alec spent all of ten minutes quizzing me, and when I told him I'd spent my time in a basement, he dismissed me, ordering me to be ready for seven. The only people I have had contact with since arriving at his apartment work for him.

And now, as he parades me on his arm like a proud husband, I want to run away. So, when I come face-to-face with Pit, I bite my inner cheek so hard, it bleeds. I allow the metallic taste to fill my mouth and breathe slow, in through my nose, out through my nose. *In. Out. In. Out.*

I didn't expect to ever see him again. That was the plan —live with Alec and forget what happened, then save enough money to leave London.

"Gentlemen, this is my wife, Tessa, although I'm sure you're all aware." He laughs, not caring that the rest of us stand awkwardly, unamused.

"You wanted us here, so here we are," says Axel bluntly. "Don't waste my fucking time with shit jokes."

"Relax," says Alec, smiling wide. "Can I get you drinks?"

"No. Where's Oleg?"

"He'll be here."

"Where are we exactly?" snaps Grizz.

"This is a charity ball. You've probably not attended many."

"Why are we here?" demands Axel.

Alec smirks. "I have my safety, and that of my wife, to think about."

Although my eyes are fixed to the ground, I can feel Pit glaring at me. I can sense the utter hatred he has for me, and I wonder what Axel told him.

"I need the bathroom," I mutter close to Alec's ear.

"I'm sorry, my darling, but I can't let you out of my sight while these feral idiots are roaming."

"Don't think I won't end your life right here, Alec," Axel hisses. "Get me Pavel Oleg, now."

"Which one was it, firecracker?" Alec asks, and I look at him blankly. "Which one took you?" My eyes betray me, going to Pit, who is still glaring at me. "Of course. He looks like the muscle." This time, I don't look away. Pit has no right to be angry with me, and I have no need to be ashamed. I had every right to leave. "Did you fuck her?" asks Alec, and I almost choke on my own breath.

"I already told you no," I hiss, pulling my arm from his.

Alec's hand dashes out, snatching my wrist and hauling me against him. I see Pit move from the corner of my eye, but Axel stops him, shaking his head in warning. "I wasn't asking you," Alec growls before turning back to Pit.

"No," says Pit firmly.

"Why?"

"Because I don't fuck whiney, sneaky, little bitches," he says coldly. His words pierce my already fragile heart as Alec's laugh rings out.

Another man joins us, shaking hands with Alec. "This is Pavel Oleg," says Alec smugly. "Pavel, meet your new suppliers."

"Let's find an office," says Pavel, shaking hands with the bikers.

We're led up some stairs and into a reception area that leads to an office. Alec turns to me. "Stay here," he says, pointing to a chair like I'm his fucking lapdog. The rest of them go into the office.

I wait for the door to close before heading back down the stairs. *Fuck him*. I'm not a prisoner anymore.

I head for the bar. "A martini," I tell the bartender. "Put it on Alec Clay's tab."

IT'S ALMOST an hour before they reappear. I see Alec scanning the room, and when his eyes land on me, I hold up my glass and smile. *Prick.*

He begins a conversation with Pavel, turning his back to me. As the bikers leave, Pit stops, and despite Axel's protests, he heads over. "Not even a goodbye," he says, his mouth close to my ear.

I shudder. "I bet you've snuck out a million times on a woman."

He laughs. "Yeah, but never one I've cared about."

"Stop kidding yourself," I say. "This time next week, you'll have someone new in your bed and I'll be just a distant memory."

"True," he says, making eye contact. "Only I didn't want to wait for the bed to get cold. London filled it nicely." And he turns and walks away.

I stare after him with tears in my eyes. What did I expect? A declaration of love? I hurt him, and now, he's paying me back.

Alec comes over. "Drink up. We have business to attend to."

When I don't drink fast enough, he takes the glass from me, spilling some of the contents down my front and slamming it on the bar. He takes my hand and practically drags me from the building.

Outside, he tugs me to him. "I saw the way he was looking at you," he spits, and I'm shocked by his sudden change in mood.

"Huh?"

"You expect me to believe there was nothing?" His

hand goes to my throat and he squeezes. "We're about to find out who's telling the truth."

He releases me and tugs me down the steps. I catch a glimpse of a car slowly pulling away, Pit is staring out the window, his hand pressed to it and his expression pained. I'm so distracted, I don't see Alec's fist until a blinding pain splinters through my head and my knees weaken, almost dropping me to the floor. "And if you've lied, it's going to be a long night."

CHAPTER 13

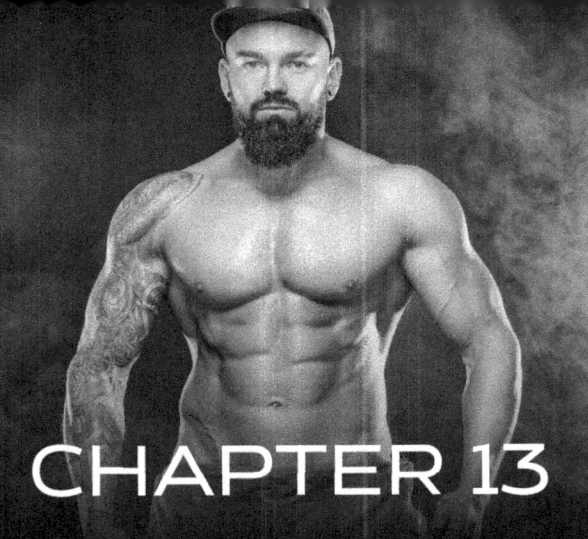

PIT

"It's not our problem," yells Axel as I slam my fist against the window.

"He's fucking hurting her," I shout. "Turn the car around." We're already in a line of traffic, but all I can see is the image of Tessa as his fist connected with her face.

"He's right," says Grizz. "Turn around."

"And risk our deal?"

"Fuck the deal," I roar.

"We have to shift the fucking gear," he yells. "I can't keep hold of it any longer. If we get caught, we're all gonna end up inside."

I bury my head in my hands. "She thinks I fucked London," I mutter. "Shit."

"Who told her that?" asks Grizz.

"I did," I spit. "I was pissed with her fucking dismissing me."

"You could've saved us all the headache if you'd have just told us how you felt," snaps Axel.

"The deal was more important to you," I remind him bitterly.

"Fuck you, Pit," he snaps. "I asked you outright, and you lied. I ain't begging for truths. I had a tough call and I chose the club, like I always do."

"Hero," I mutter.

Axel swerves the car, taking a corner too fast before slamming on the brakes and jumping out. "Fuck," mutters Grizz, unfastening his seatbelt. "Now, you've done it."

Axel pulls my door open. "Get out." I do, too tired to argue and too exhausted to care. "If you've got something to say, big man, say it."

"You care about the money," I spit.

"Half a mill is a lot," he snaps. "But I don't give a shit about that if it means you're suffering."

"Bullshit," I argue. "You knew I was falling."

"And I asked you."

"What was I meant to say?"

"The fucking truth," he bellows in my face. "Pres, I like her and I can't let her go. But you said you wanted the road. You said you couldn't settle, it wasn't for you. So, I put the club first. I chose to offload those guns so we can all breathe again. You know the sentence if we get caught with that shit? I've never held onto that amount for longer than a week. That's what we do. We buy, we sell, we move it. That's why people deal with us. We're quick and reliable." He shoves me hard. "I asked you not to get involved with her. I told you we were gonna make a deal."

"I didn't plan on it," I yell.

"If we could all just calm the fuck down," says Grizz,

stepping between us. "I have a solution." He holds up a piece of paper between his fingers. "Turns out, Pavel Oleg doesn't trust Alec either. He slipped me this with his phone number on. I assume he'd like a call."

Axel snatches it, opening it and staring wide-eyed. "Why the fuck didn't you say?"

"Because I didn't want Romeo to fuck anything up in there. We have to call him and check he's on the same page. If I'd have said anything there, Mister Muscle here would've crushed Alec's skull, and what if I've got it wrong?"

"Call him," I snap, getting back in the car.

"Let's wait until morning," says Grizz. "We don't want to appear too eager."

"What about Tessa?" I demand.

"She's faced worse, right? What's a day going to do?"

TESSA

The pain is blinding, literally. White lights dance in my eyes and my face throbs. I feel my legs dangling off the edge of the bed, and I try to drag myself higher, giving up when dizziness takes over. "Not so fast, firecracker," hisses Alec, and I breathe a sigh of relief when he unzips my dress, thankful that the crushing of my ribs is easing. He tugs it down my body, almost pulling me off the bed, and then his face comes into view. He leers down at me, and I feel my hands being lifted above my head. "Tie them," he says to someone else, then he's back to leering at me while my hands are pinned above my head and tied in place. I frown, unable to work out what's happening. My head feels fuzzy. "Don't worry, you'll come back fighting soon enough. The drug is wearing off."

Drug? I have a faint recollection of Alec placing a cloth over my face when we were in the car coming home.

Alec pulls my underwear from my body, and as much as I want to protest, I have no energy. And then his fingers are inside me, and I wince. It's uncomfortable and sore, but he doesn't stop when he notices my facial expressions. "I paid a lot of money," he whispers in my ear, "and I better get what I paid for."

I scream when he pushes his erection into me, and suddenly, I don't feel as fuzzy. I try to kick out, and he laughs, digging his fingers into my thighs. "That's it, firecracker, show me how much you want me." As my vision comes back, I glance around the room to find another man watching. Alec pulls from me and looks down, inspecting between my legs. "Would you look at that," he says calmly, "not a fucking drop."

"I don't know what you mean?" I rush the words out, sounding desperate.

"Jason, take over."

Alec steps back, and the other man gets into position, unfastening his trousers. "No," I yell, thrashing around to try and free myself. "Please, no," I scream as he pins me to the bed.

"You lied to me, firecracker. I'm about to make your life hell."

∼

I WAKE AND GROAN ALOUD. My body aches, and I already feel the swelling in both eyes and my lips. My wrists are sore from the ropes, and I try once again to loosen them to no avail. I push to sit up and wince as more pain shoots through my body.

"Ready for round six . . . or was it seven? I've lost count."

Alec is sitting in the armchair watching me. He's still naked, and I shudder with repulsion. I remember seeing his body when he sent me pictures online. His muscles and toned abs had me reeling. Now, they disgust me. "Jason had some work to get on with, but I can find a replacement if you'd like?" I'd never thought about having two men at once. It just hadn't crossed my mind. And after last night, I don't ever want it to happen again.

"Don't pretend you're some shy little virgin, Tessa. We both know it isn't true."

"I am," I lie. I've been saying the same thing all night.

"But your body responded like a pro," he mocks.

"I can't help my body's reaction," I spit angrily.

"Maybe we should try more men?" he muses. "Three, maybe four?"

"No," I say firmly, bringing the sheets tighter around my body.

He sneers. "Oh, this isn't your game, Tessa. It's mine. I decide who and how many."

I begin to sob. "Please, Alec. This wasn't what I wanted."

He laughs loudly. "You sold yourself to a stranger on the internet. Were you expecting me to be a decent man?"

I'm once again reminded how naïve I've been and humiliation burns me. "I have a special guest arriving shortly," he adds, standing. "You haven't seen him for a while." I frown as he heads for the door. "Get some rest."

∼

I MUST NOD OFF, but I wake with a start to find Alec sneering down at me with his hand around my throat. "Are you ready for your surprise, firecracker?" I shake my head, and he grins. "Of course, you are." He grips a handful of my hair and pulls my head up to look into the eyes I know so well. "Steven," I whisper. Horror fills me when his smile is just as evil as I remember.

"The one and only."

"I'll let you get reacquainted," says Alec, heading for the door. "Keep her in one piece. Those bikers might pull the deal if they realise she's gone too soon."

Steven Kendal sits on the bed. He's bigger now, his shoulders wider and his arms muscly. "It's been a while."

"What are you doing here?"

"What do you think?" he asks, running his hand up my inner thigh. I try to move, but he pins me in place. "Don't be shy, Tessa. I've waited years for this."

"Jesus," I cry. "Have you been holding a grudge all this time? We were fucking kids, Steven."

"And now we're adults."

Tears leak from my eyes. "Haven't you moved on, gotten married?"

"I'm not here for a happy reunion, Tessa. You were a fucking bitch to me."

My mouth falls open in shock. "You hated me. You made my life hell."

"Because you looked down your nose at me, thinking you were too fucking good."

"I didn't," I say, barely believing his words. "I was terrified of you. You bullied me."

He laughs. "Now, now, let's not make me the villain. I tried to befriend you, and you made it impossible."

"Because I wouldn't have sex with you?" I scoff. "Christ, shit happens. Move on."

He stands. "That would be easy if I wasn't so affected by you. I saw your little ad online," he says, unfastening his belt, "selling yourself like a prostitute."

I gasp. "You saw it?"

"I'm married, so I couldn't follow through completely. That's when my brother stepped in." My throat tightens. "And then it all got messy. And now, Alec tells me you're not a fucking virgin?"

"I am . . . I was. He took that away," I cry.

Steven climbs onto the bed, fisting his erection. "I told him to have his fun. What was the point in keeping you untouched if you weren't . . . untouched?"

"Oh my god, you've been behind this all along?"

"Firecracker," he says, winking. He lines himself up at my entrance. "And now, I have my very own toy to play with whenever I feel like it."

PIT

We file into church and take our seats. "I called our Russian dealer. He's willing to cut the middleman out," says Axel with a wide smile. "Apparently, he doesn't like or trust Alec or his brother, Steven." The name strikes something inside me.

"Steven?" I repeat.

"Yep. Apparently, they're adopted brothers, crazy and reckless. He doesn't want them involved at all and actually offered us more of a cut if we didn't use them."

"Have you got a name?" I ask, frowning. "A full one?"

Axel takes out a piece of paper and throws it on the table. "I'm running checks on them both," he tells me as I take it and stare at the names.

Steven Kendal.

"Jesus," I mutter, throwing it back on the table. "He bullied Tessa when she was younger."

Axel's frown deepens. "There could be more than one Steven Kendal."

"But what are the chances? He was cruel to her. There's every chance this could be a vendetta."

"Okay, well, the second I get the addresses, we'll head out. We're ending Alec for pulling the shit with our guns in the first place. It makes no difference if we take out his brother too."

Relief floods me, and I nod in agreement. Knowing I'll have Tessa back with me brings a sense of calm.

⁓

IT'S another few hours before we get an address for Steven and I'm standing outside the pristine house. "She's not here," I mutter.

"How do you know?" asks Grizz.

"It's my job to know. The house is too nice. The neighbourhood is too quiet. He wouldn't bring her here."

"So, let's knock and ask," says Axel, walking up the path.

A woman answers cradling a baby. Both her eyes are bruised and she looks exhausted. She eyes us warily. "Yes?"

"We're looking for Steven."

"He's out."

"Do you know where?" asks Axel. She gives her head a shake. "Anything you can tell us would be helpful."

"I don't even know you," she mutters, gently stroking her baby's head.

"No, but looking at you, I'd say you could do with our help," I cut in. "If we find him, it might relieve you of a troublesome life."

She bites her lower lip, thinking over my words. "Let me get my phone," she offers, heading back inside.

She returns, holding it out to us. It shows a map with Steven's location. I smile, snapping a picture. "Thank you."

"I didn't help you," she says. "He can't know."

I give a nod. "Same goes, you never saw us before, we were never here." And we head out.

∼

THE APARTMENT IS in a nice area, but it's lacking security, and as I scan the labels for the doorbell, I smile. "Alec," I say, pressing the buzzer for his neighbour, and a man answers. "Hey, man, it's Alec from next door. I forgot my key. Can you let me in?"

The door clicks, and I pull it open. Grizz slaps me on the back. "I forgot what a buzz it is to be out with you."

We take the elevator, stepping out onto the landing and listening for any sign there's someone here. After a minute, Grizz takes the lead, gently turning the handle to the door. It's locked, like we expected, so I knock hard. "Delivery," I call out, pressing a finger over the spy hole.

After a moment, there's a voice on the other side of the door. "I didn't order."

"Erm . . . it's for Alec," I say, sounding confused.

"Fuck's sake," I hear him mutter before the lock clicks and the door is yanked open. "I said I—"

I shove the door back, taking Alec by surprise. Grizz takes hold of him, slamming him against the wall. I continue through the apartment, pushing doors open as I pass, and then I hear her. She's crying out, like she's in pain, and I run towards the sound, shoving open the last door and filling the doorway. There on the bed is Tessa, and between her open legs is a man. I can already see the bruises on her inner thighs and blood smeared there. A painful roar rips from me as I grab him by his neck and drag him from her. She immediately scrambles towards the head of the bed, tucking her knees to her chest.

My chest heaves with anger, my throat tightening with each breath. "Name?" I bark.

He sneers. "You're fucking up my plans," he says calmly.

I squeeze harder, and he winces. "Wrong answer," I

growl, pulling a blade from my jacket and holding it under his eye. "I'm guessing you're Steven."

"You've done your homework."

I press the tip of the blade to the soft skin, nicking it and watching the blood bead to the surface. "Te, are you okay?" I call out, not taking my eyes from the monster before me. A sob escapes her, and I press the knife into the flesh under his eye. He grits his teeth, refusing to let me hear his pain as blood drips from the wound. I drag it out slowly.

"Why do you even fucking care?" he grits out, spittle flying from his mouth. "You were only holding her to get to Alec."

Axel appears in the doorway. "Why's he still talking?"

"You're right," I mutter, gripping the blade tightly and shoving it up through his jaw. I savour the feel as it slices through the skin and then through his tongue. I twist it, and he begins to choke, grabbing my wrist with both his hands. I shove the blade one last time, piercing his brain, watching as the life leaves his eyes.

He slumps, his knees giving out, and I release him so he hits the floor hard. "Piece of shit," I mutter, spitting on him.

Axel gives a slight nod to the bed, and I spin to see Tessa with her head resting on her knees, sobbing quietly.

I wipe my hands down my jeans and move towards her. I lower onto the bed, and she jumps in fright. "It's just me," I reassure her. "I'm going to untie you," I add, carefully reaching for the ropes. They're tied tightly, and Axel sees me struggling and passes me his own knife. I cut through the binds and release her. She rubs her wrists, which look red raw, and I clench my jaw in anger.

I take off my shirt and wrap it around her shoulders. "Let's take you home," I tell her, sliding my arms under her legs and around her back, lifting her into my arms. I feel the way she stiffens, but she doesn't protest, so I carry her from the room and out the apartment.

CHAPTER 14

TESSA

I can't shake the images of Steven Kendal from my mind. The way he sneered as he took what he wanted from me. I shudder, wrapping my arms tighter around myself.

The bedroom door opens and Lexi pops her head in, offering a small smile. It's sad, like she knows everything, and I hate that. It makes me feel more exposed. "How are you doing?" she asks, then she winces and steps farther into the room. "Stupid question, sorry."

I rest my chin on my raised knees. I've always hated uncomfortable silences, but since coming back to this clubhouse just a few hours ago, I can't muster up the words I need, not even to settle the questions Pit kept throwing my way.

Lexi sits on the edge of the bed. "Look, I know you must be in hell right now, but Pit's going out of his mind with worry. Do you need anything? Food? Water?" I stare at the opposite wall. *How can I eat a damn thing when I feel so sick?* "Okay, maybe I'll just bring you something, a biscuit even?" *And why the hell should I push myself to ease Pit's guilt?* Fuck him.

I close my eyes, relief flooding me when I feel her get up from the bed and leave the room. I picture my mum sitting on her bed, combing her curly hair. I feel my lips lifting into a smile as I recall the softness of her voice. Sometimes, I had to really listen hard to hear her because she was so softly spoken.

My mum tips her head, smiling my way as she scrunches her curls into a bounce. And then I hear him, and her smile fades. She shoves her brush into the drawer and stands quickly, grabbing my hand and pulling me to the wardrobe. I frown as she shoves me inside, throwing clothes over me to bury me and slamming the door.

I hear my breaths coming in rapid spurts and my heart hammering loudly in my chest. My ears get that whooshing sound until I can just about make out yelling. I jump in fright at the sound of flesh hitting flesh and my mum crying as he lays into her.

"Tessa? Tessa?" My hands are being pulled from my ears, and I open my eyes, staring directly into Pit's concerned ones. "Shit, are you okay?"

I take a steadying breath and pull my wrists free from his grip. "The dark," I mutter, frowning. "She used to hide me in the dark." And then my tears fall as large sobs wrack my body.

Pit pulls me to him, wrapping his arms around me. "You're okay," he soothes, "I'm here."

His words bring me back to reality, and I disentangle myself from him, wiping my eyes with my hands. I shuffle to the edge of the bed and push to stand. "I want to leave."

Pit looks alarmed. "And go where?"

"I don't know," I whisper. "Away from here."

"Tessa, it's late. Sleep on it."

"Sleep?" I scoff. "You think I can sleep?"

"No," he says, shaking his head. "Probably not. So, just sit. I'll sit with you. And when the sun comes up, we'll talk about it."

I lower back onto the bed and twist my fingers together. "How did you find me?"

"I remembered his name," he tells me. "Steven's. And when Axel mentioned him, I realised what might be going on. We paid his wife a visit, and she shared his location."

"You remembered," I whisper. I'd only mentioned his name briefly, but Pit had remembered.

"I'd committed it to memory," he says bitterly.

"Why?"

He fixes me with serious eyes. "Cos I was always gonna make him pay, Te."

More bloodshed. I want to be mad at his threat. But how can I be? He would have taken Steven out for me. "What if I'm pregnant?" I whisper, the fear of that thought gripping me. "What if I'm pregnant with his kid?"

Pit stands abruptly, his fists clenched by his sides. "I'll get the doctor." And he storms out.

Minutes later, Luna comes in. She's holding a vase with some bright flowers in. "Gemma chose them," she mutters, placing them on the side. "Pit asked me to keep you company." My heart sinks. He's probably disgusted being near me, knowing I let them do what they did to me. "I think he just needs a minute to cool off," she adds.

"He hates me," I mutter, wiping my wet cheeks. "I don't blame him."

"He doesn't hate you," she rushes to reassure me. "You confirmed his worst fears, and now, he wants to kill the bastard all over again."

I bury my face in my hands. "They didn't use protection," I whisper, "and all I can think about is what if I'm pregnant, or what if they've given me some fucking disease. All those years of being careful and protecting myself to end up like this."

She gently rubs my back. "I know it doesn't feel like it right now, Tessa, but the memories will fade a little and their scent will go. You'll stop feeling their hands on you and things will just feel less . . . bad."

I glance at her, and there's a faraway look in her eyes. "It happened to you?"

She blinks, shaking her head like she's clearing her thoughts, and she forces a smile. "Like I said, it gets easier. Just take one day at a time."

"I'll never be able to trust a man again," I mumble.

She takes my hand and squeezes it. "You will. I promise."

"How long did it take you?" I ask.

"To trust?" She thinks over my question. "A while," she admits. "Grizz wasn't easy to trust at first, but he stuck around and that's what counts. Pit will too," she says, smiling. "He'll get you through this."

I'm already shaking my head. "I don't want him to. I was better off when it was just me," I tell her. "I thought I needed a man for stability, but it turns out I don't."

She pulls her legs under her, getting comfortable. "What did you do before all this happened?"

"I had a cute little one-bed flat," I say, smiling at the memory. "I worked a nine-to-five job."

"Were you happy?"

I wasn't, not at all. The routine I'd found myself stuck in was becoming tedious and boring. It's why I stepped out of my comfort zone—I wanted to get a life. Turns out a life isn't all it's cracked up to be. "Yes," I lie.

"So, have you still got your flat?"

I shake my head. "I was renting and the lease was up. The owners were selling it."

"What about money?"

I shake my head again. "I didn't have a lot of that either. The flat cost a lot to rent."

"But you married, right?" I nod. "So, whatever he had will be yours?"

Hope swells in my chest. "Maybe."

"Well, of course, it will be. I'll speak to Grizz and get him to talk to Axel."

PIT

I pace, inhaling a lungful of air to try to calm my racing thoughts. The second Tessa confirmed what I already knew, I saw nothing but darkness. I guess a part of me was hoping I'd walked in at exactly the right time, saving her from their disgusting hands. I was naïve to even hope they hadn't spent the last twenty-four hours hurting her in ways I don't want to imagine.

Fletch steps out holding a bottle of Jack, which I take from him, downing a few mouthfuls. "Luna's got this weird idea that Tessa might gain something from all this." I pause my pacing to stare at him. "If Alec has assets, they'll transfer over to his wife, right?" I narrow my eyes. He's got a point. "Anyway, Axel's called church." And he heads inside.

I follow a few seconds later, taking my chair while still clutching the bottle of whiskey. Axel takes it from me, passing it to Grizz, who dumps it on the table behind him. "It's not gonna help," he adds with a shrug.

"Is Luna right?" I ask. "Will Tessa get everything?"

Axel gives a stiff shake of the head, and my heart sinks a little. "He's about to be dropped into the Thames with a weight tied to his neck. That fucker won't surface for years, and until then, he's not classed as dead. Even if she reported him missing, she'd have to answer a shitload of questions. According to Gemma, it's not worth risking."

"Besides," Coop adds, sliding a file towards me, "I did some digging, and he doesn't have much."

I open it and stare at the negative figure on the bank statement. "It was never a real deal," I mutter, slamming it closed. "He was just getting her for his stepbrother."

"Fucking sick bastards," says Coop.

"How is she doing?" Axel asks.

"Like shit. She won't talk. The doc's given her the morning after pill," I say bitterly, "and he took swabs and bloods to check for fucking HIV and shit."

"Luna thinks you should take her back to the farmhouse," says Grizz. "She's not ready to be surrounded by a bunch of men she doesn't trust."

"He's got a point," agrees Axel.

"She wants to leave," I mutter, scrubbing my hands over my tired face. "I convinced her to stay tonight, but she's set on leaving tomorrow."

"She's not ready," says Coop.

"Tell me about it," I mutter. "Can I go?" I ask, and Axel gives a nod. I push to my feet. "Thanks for helping tonight," I add. "I know everything you've done is for me."

I get to the bedroom and pause outside. The unfamiliar feeling of nerves flutters in my stomach, and I inwardly groan. I push the door open and inhale sharply at the sight of Tessa curled up asleep with King stretched out beside her and Gigi on the floor at the foot of the bed.

I shrug out of my kutte and place it on the hook on the back of the door, then I slip off my boots and take a seat in the reclining chair. King lifts his head, assessing me, and for a second, I think he's going to growl, but he settles again. I scoff, but deep down, I'm pleased he's guarding her. He senses she needs it.

~

I WAKE with a start and sit bolt upright. The bed is empty and panic fills me as I push to stand. King is at the French door whimpering, and I make out her figure standing on the balcony. "Easy," I whisper, stroking King's head. "Go lie down." And he does.

I slide the door open and step out. "It's cold out here," I say, pulling off my shirt. I place it over her shoulders, and she takes the edges and pulls it around herself. "Couldn't sleep?"

She shakes her head. "Yet I'm so tired."

"I can ask the doc for some sleeping tablets?"

She shakes her head. "No, I don't want to face the nightmares."

"You can't stay awake forever," I say with a small smile. "How about I lay beside you?" She's already staring at me in horror, and I hold my hands up, feeling like a dick. "I didn't mean . . ." I sigh heavily. "I sleep better when you're beside me," I admit. "I thought it might help. I didn't mean anything."

Her expression relaxes and tears fill her eyes. "See what they've done, making me think everyone wants one thing?"

"You've been to hell and back," I say, "and I haven't helped in that."

"Being with them almost made me thankful for being with you." She scoffs. "How fucked-up is that? I went from one prison to another."

"If I could take it back . . ." I mutter, gripping the rail tightly.

"Maybe I can get my old job back," she says, staring out into the night sky.

"What did you do?"

She smiles. "I was just a receptionist, nothing special."

"Hey, don't put yourself down," I scold. "Every job is important."

"They've probably hired someone now anyway."

"I could ask around, see if the club needs anyone."

She laughs, but it's empty. "I don't think that's a good idea."

"We're not bad," I say, wincing. "At least, they're not."

"Axel told you to take me and keep me locked up while he cut a deal."

"He was protecting the club."

"I guess it's hard to see any wrongdoing when you're in his protected circle."

"Ask Lexi or Luna, even Gemma. They all had some kind of run-in with the club. Lexi and Gemma were coppers trying to take us down."

"They crossed the club," she snaps, "I didn't."

"You're right," I say, nodding. "But after everything, they stayed and became part of the club. Would they do that if it was so bad?"

She rolls her eyes. "I can't stand here while you tell me how wonderful your precious club is. Not after everything."

"Where will you go when you leave?" I demand.

"I have no idea, but anywhere away from here." And she heads back inside.

CHAPTER 15

TESTA

Two days have passed and I haven't mentioned leaving again. I'm a hypocrite, I know it, but the thought of stepping outside these walls and into the unknown is scary. So, when Pit comes into the room holding out some new trainers for me, I eye them warily. "Put these on."

"Why?"

"Trust me." I scoff, and he relents. "Okay, don't trust me, whatever, just put them on. I have a surprise."

"I don't like surprises," I mutter, pushing my feet into the trainers and standing.

He takes me by the hand and leads me downstairs. I feel like everyone's eyes are on me as we pass through the main room and head outside. He stops by his bike and pulls out the spare helmet before putting on his own. He senses I'm hesitant. The last time we did this, he took me to a murder scene. I shudder, and he smiles sadly. "It's a good surprise, I promise."

I get on behind him and the bike jumps to life. We ride

for ten minutes before he's stopping outside a small semi-detached house. I climb off and hand him my helmet, looking around and taking in the quiet street. I follow him up the path, where he produces a set of keys and unlocks the door.

Inside, the place is beautiful. It's cosy, with a lived-in look. "What are we doing here?" I ask.

He holds out the keys to me, and I frown. "It's yours," he tells me.

I gasp. "What?"

"I'm not saying you have to leave the club. In fact, when you do, I'll be . . . well, it's your choice," he mutters, "but when you're ready, I wanted you to have a place you can call home."

"You bought me a house?"

He nods. "It's safe here. The street is mainly nosey old people, and it's a cul-de-sac, so no traffic will flow through. There's a top-of-the-range house alarm as well as a panic alarm connected right to the police."

"Why would I need a panic alarm?" I ask, my mind reeling with questions.

"You won't, but I wanted you to feel safe."

"Pit, this is all too much," I mutter, not taking the keys.

He places them on the side. "At least take a look around."

"I can't live in a house owned by you," I snap.

He pulls an envelope out from his jacket pocket. "I don't own it, Tessa, you do."

I stare wide-eyed. "Why would you do that?"

He shrugs. "Guilt. An apology. I dunno, Tess. All I know is I need you to be happy."

"I can't take this," I say firmly. "You've lost your mind."

"I think . . ." he begins, pausing and sighing, "I think I've fallen in love with you." I freeze as the words pour from him, my mouth slightly ajar. "And I know you don't feel that way about me, and after everything, I don't ever expect you to feel that way. But I need you to forgive me, Tessa. What I did to you was terrible, and I can't sleep properly or even eat because the guilt is ripping me apart."

I want to forgive him. My mind is screaming at me to tell him that I think I feel the same, but my heart aches. I've seen the man he is and I can't be a part of that. I take the envelope and give a slight nod. "I'll stay here for a short while until I get back on my feet. But I don't want your house, Pit." I pause before adding, "And I don't want you."

He briefly closes his eyes before pressing his lips into a firm line and nodding in acceptance. He heads for the door. "Look around. I just need some air."

I take my time walking around the property. It's freshly decorated in creams and light greys. It's bright, and every room has a huge vase of flowers. When I finally step outside, Pit is sitting on his bike with his helmet in place. When I stop beside him, he lifts the visor and forces a smile that doesn't quite reach his eyes. "All good?" he asks.

I nod. "It's kitted out with everything I could ever need," I say.

"Yeah, I had the women do all that. It's not really my area."

I smile gratefully. "So, I was thinking, maybe I could stay here now, as in today."

My words sink in and his expression tells me how hurt he is, but he nods anyway. "Great idea."

"And I have a panic button in case I get scared," I say with a small laugh.

He pulls out my mobile phone and hands it to me. I hadn't even bothered with it since I went back to the clubhouse. "My number is in there," he tells me. "Anything, no matter how small, just call or text me."

"Right."

He then pulls out his own mobile. "The pictures," he mutters, and he shows me the photos of me on my knees by the dead body, "I don't need them." And then he proceeds to delete them one by one.

"I appreciate it," I say, unsure how to feel about it. "And this isn't goodbye, right? I mean, you're gonna be my landlord for a short amount of time."

He gives a stiff nod. "Yeah."

"So, I'll be in touch."

He starts the bike and flips the visor down. I watch as he turns the bike and speeds away. Why does it feel so final?

∼

I DON'T KNOW why I thought this would be easy alone. As I sit in my new bedroom, with the small lamp glowing and tears soaking my cheeks, I realise this is the first time I've been properly alone in months. It's almost two in the morning and I've lost count of the times I've picked up my mobile to call Pit but then slammed it back down and gave myself a pep talk. I'm a grown woman, and I have to do this because whether I like it or not, I'm all alone in this world.

My mobile vibrates across the dresser, and I jump with fright. Reaching for it, I see it's a text from Pit, and my heart immediately speeds up.

> Pit: Goodnight, sweet dreams, Tess x

I smile as more tears blur my vision. Surely, if he texted me first, it doesn't count, right?

> Me: I wish. I can't sleep. X

His response is immediate.

> Pit: Me either. Fancy company? X

I hold the phone to my chest for a second. I *do* want company. *Badly.* It's my first night, and I can be more independent tomorrow.

> Me: Okay x

> Pit: I'm outside x

I frown, slipping from my bed and grabbing a shirt I'd stolen from Pit. I rush downstairs and unlock the door to find him already there with his hands stuffed in his pockets, looking sheepish. I smirk. "Ummm, stalker much?"

"Guilty as charged," he murmurs as I open the door

wider for him to come inside. "I brought gifts," he adds, picking a bag up from the floor. "Hot chocolate powder and milk."

My frown deepens. "And you just happened to be in the area with that stuff?"

He grins, heading for the kitchen. "I went for a ride cos I couldn't sleep. Stopped at the twenty-four-hour shop to grab these and headed here in the hope you'd be awake to keep me company."

I take a seat at the table while Pit sets about heating the milk in a pan and adding the chocolate powder. "How come you couldn't sleep?" I ask.

He shrugs. "A lot on my mind."

"Me too."

He pours the hot chocolate into two mugs and joins me at the table. "Maybe speaking to someone would help?"

"Maybe," I say, "but the thought of telling a complete stranger everything that happened . . ." I shudder. "I just wanna forget about it."

"I'm so fucking pissed," he eventually says, meeting my eyes. "Killing them once wasn't enough. I wanna do it over and over again."

I reach across and place my hand over his. "I'm glad they're dead."

"They didn't suffer enough."

"I just have to find a way to move on."

"How?" he asks, shaking his head slightly and staring down at his mug. "How the fuck can you move on from that shit?"

I shrug. "I don't know. Luna said it all fades with time. Eventually, I won't feel them or smell them." Pit's fists tighten around his mug. "But they're the last men to have touched me," I add, feeling shame wash over me. "How do I erase that?" I bite my lower lip, scared to make the proposition that's on the tip of my tongue. I take a breath. "Maybe if we . . . yah know, if we just . . ."

His head shoots up, his eyes wide. "No," he says bluntly, and I immediately recoil like he's slapped me.

"Oh god, I'm so sorry," I rush to say, feeling even more disgusting.

Pit practically jumps out his chair and rushes to me, grabbing my hands in his and kneeling before me. His eyes search my own. "Te, I didn't mean I don't want to—of course, I do—but it's too soon, and who knows what will trigger you?"

I push to stand, and he drops my hands. "It's lack of sleep," I say, forcing a laugh to lighten the mood. "But I feel much sleepier after the drink and . . ." I shrug again. "Maybe you should go."

He stands too but doesn't move out of my space. "Don't do that," he whispers, hooking a finger around mine. "I'm not rejecting you."

I nod. "I know. I just feel so embarrassed right now," I mutter. "Make it easier on me."

"You don't need to feel embarrassed. Your emotions are all over the place, it's not surprising."

"Still, I'd rather die of embarrassment alone," I say with an awkward smile.

He gives a nod and heads for the door. I follow, willing my cheeks to stop burning. "Goodnight," he whispers, cupping my jaw and lightly kissing me on the forehead. A friendly kiss, just to make his message clear.

"Goodnight," I say, avoiding eye contact.

PIT

It's not how I wanted to leave things. I didn't expect her to say what she said, but fuck, I get it—she doesn't want those fuckers to be the last ones who touched her. And, for whatever reason, she trusts me. Fuck knows why after everything I've done.

"Did you go and see her?" asks Axel from his office as I pass.

I pause, leaning in the doorway and shaking my head. "Couldn't bring myself to tell her, Pres."

I don't miss the sympathetic look on his face. "Maybe text her when you've gone?"

I give a stiff nod and head upstairs. Axel was right about one thing—I need to hit the road. The anger and pain inside me will result in a shitstorm, and I can't put Tessa through any more. She needs to find her own way with people just like her, who have families and meet friends for dinner. I can't give her the stability she needs, and I certainly won't ask her to sacrifice her dreams for me.

∼

I TOSS and turn for the remainder of the darkness, and the second the sun rises, I get up and take the dogs for a walk. For the first time, I'm leaving them both behind, and I hate that, but right now, I just need to take care of me.

When I get back to the clubhouse, I head into church, where Axel is keen to get started. "We all know Pit hates being around us," he jokes, and some of the men laugh. "Today, he's hitting the road and who the fuck knows when we'll see him again. He's leaving his crazy dogs behind, and the prospects will take care of them. And as usual, any work you've got outside the area, run it by me and we'll send it Pit's way."

Once church is over, I shake hands with my brothers, and they take turns wishing me well. And then I find King and Gigi, burying my face in their furry necks to say goodbye. Usually, I'd be back in a couple months, but right now, I don't know how I feel about coming back.

~

I'VE BEEN on the road for six hours when I finally stop and pull into a hotel. Just being alone with my thoughts is already making me feel better. Once I'm in the room, I pull out my mobile and turn it on. It beeps twice, and I open the messages from Tessa.

> Tessa: Pit, I'm so sorry. I feel mortified whenever I think about it. I just wanted you to know I'm not some sex pest or a freak. I just needed normal and you gave me that. Sorry x

> Tessa: Now I'm overthinking. Are you avoiding me? Oh god, do you hate me because of it? I'm so ashamed. x

I smile. Trust her to overthink everything.

Me: Relax, we're cool, Tessa. X

Her reply is almost instant, like she's been waiting for my message.

> Tessa: I got out the house today. I went to the shop all by myself. I didn't even cry once. I hope you're proud of me. I am. X

My heart twists. I am proud. So fucking proud. But also worried. Because every time we text, I feel myself wanting her more. I turn my phone off and chuck it on the side. I need sleep, because tomorrow, I'm heading for Ireland.

CHAPTER 16

TESSA

It's been a week. A week since Pit replied to my message. A week since I saw him. *A week.* And honestly, it feels like a lifetime. I miss him.

I'm so lost in thought, it's not until the flash of black startles me that I realise King is running towards me. I laugh as he pushes me onto my back and licks my face. "Okay," I giggle, pushing him away, "not the face."

"Heel." King immediately runs back to the voice, and as I sit up, I'm sad to see it's not Pit walking him but one of the men from the club. "Sorry 'bout that," he mutters, clipping the lead onto King's collar.

"It's fine," I say, pushing to my feet and heading over so I can fuss both dogs. "Shooter, right?" He nods. "Where's Pit? I didn't think he let anyone else walk his dogs."

Shooter shifts uncomfortably. "He's not around."

I frown. "What do you mean?"

"I shouldn't really say."

"Is he okay? At least tell me he's not hurt," I say, panic lacing my words.

He scratches his head, still glancing around like he's expecting someone to jump out on him. "He hit the road."

His words surprise me, and I gasp a breath in. "Oh," I whisper. "Right. Of course. Erm, is he gone for long? It's just, I didn't think he ever left the dogs."

"He's abroad. Too much hassle to take the dogs. Take care." And he walks away, leaving me staring after him with a million questions.

I head over to the coffee hut. They give free coffee to people who need it, and as I pull a receipt off the help board and hand it to the cashier, I battle with myself not to cry. He always said he missed the road, that it was like a part of him, but I can't pretend I'm not hurt he didn't say goodbye.

I take my coffee and sit on a nearby bench, pulling my mobile out.

> Me: You left and didn't say goodbye? I guess I can't blame you. Why would you come and say goodbye? It's not like we were friends or anything.

I hit send and sigh, staring at the screen in anger.

> Me: Actually, I take that back. We were friends. We shared something special and I can't believe you'd just leave like that, Pit. You didn't even have the decency to tell me to my face. And you could've left the dogs with me. King would've been great company.

I roll my eyes at how pathetic I'm being. It was always going to be this way. And why should I care if he left? The man was crazy, right? I mean, he took me and held me captive. But he also turned out to be quite nice, in a dark and moody sort of way. Plus, he made sure I had a roof over my head. He turned out to be the only person who ever really took notice of me. He was my only friend.

"Well, you look like you have the weight of the world on your shoulders." I look up just as a man sits beside me, taking a sip of his own coffee.

"I just found out my friend left. It was a bit of a shock."

He side-eyes me, and I take a second to examine his kind face and laughter lines around his eyes. "That's shitty. I'm Lucas, by the way." He holds out a hand for me to shake, but I hesitate. After all, these sorts of random meetings never tend to work out well for me. "I don't bite," he adds with a laugh, so I reluctantly shake it.

"I'm Tessa."

"Well, Tessa, I run workshops at the local church." He retrieves a card from his inside jacket pocket and holds it out to me. "I saw you take a receipt from the board." I feel myself blush. "Hey, not judging, it's nothing to be ashamed of. We've all been there, me included. I help people find work, brush up on interview skills, that sort of thing. You're welcome to join us later at six. It's free of charge." I stare at the card. Father Lucas. *A man of God.* "I don't wear the collar," he adds, almost reading my mind, then he laughs. "It puts people off."

"I'll think about it," I tell him, tucking the card in my pocket.

He leans back, staring out over the park. "Sometimes, we attract towards people," he says. "They come into our lives for a reason. I believe we met today because you need my help."

"Maybe."

"Something tells me you haven't had much luck lately."

I scoff. "Understatement."

"Then come tonight at six." He pushes to his feet and smiles down at me. "It could be the start of your new life."

"I don't believe," I blurt out as he turns to walk away. He pauses and glances back with a small smile playing on his lips. "In God, I mean. He's never there for me, so I stopped believing a long time ago."

"But you believed at one time?"

I shrug. "I don't really know. My mother used to read stories to me from the Bible when I was a kid, but we didn't go to church or anything."

"I'll let you in on a little secret, Tessa. I didn't believe either a few years back. Then someone came along and saved me, and now, I want to do the same for you. Six o' clock." And he turns and walks away.

Maybe he's right. Maybe it's the fresh start I need. And God knows I need a job right now. I laugh to myself at my play on words. It's clearly a sign.

∞

I CHECK my reflection in the glass door before pulling it open and stepping inside. I inhale deeply, trying to calm my nerves before releasing slowly. There are a few people milling around at the front of the church, but it's nothing like I expected—it looks more like a community centre than an actual church.

Lucas spots me and excuses himself from a bunch of older ladies, heading over with a huge smile on his face. "You came," he states.

"Well, I thought I should at least find out what the fuss is about."

"Let me introduce you to everyone," he says, striding back towards the others. When he senses I'm not following, he turns back to me.

"Erm, I'm a little shy," I mutter, shrugging. "I'm not comfortable around lots of people."

He frowns slightly but nods. "That's not a problem, Tessa. We'll start slow. Come and meet my wife. She's in the office, and she's our careers expert."

I follow him into a small office where a woman is sitting behind the desk, tapping away on a laptop. She looks up when we enter and smiles warmly. I instantly relax. "Mary, this is Tessa."

"Hi, Tessa, come in, take a seat." Lucas gives me a reassuring nod, and I take a seat. He slips out, leaving us alone. "So, what brings you here tonight?"

"Erm, your husband mentioned you're a careers expert, and I really need a job."

"I can help you out there. What was your last role?"

"I've some experience in retail, and I've done some office work. Just filing and answering the telephone."

"And you have an address?" I nod, and she smiles again, tapping away on her laptop. "We've had some new jobs just come in today. How do you feel about cleaning?"

"I can clean," I say with a nod.

"We do also have a receptionist role not far from here. Are you local to this area?"

"Five minutes up the road."

"Do you have a curriculum vitae?" I shake my head. "Let's get that sorted first, then we can apply for some of these positions."

∼

BY THE TIME I leave almost two hours later, I am smiling from ear to ear. Mary and Lucas made me feel so much more positive about my future, and once I have some money coming in, I can pay rent to Pit and even find my own place and move out.

I get home and shower. I don't have many outfits, so I get into my pyjamas and put my clothes straight in the washing machine. Mary helped me fill out an application for financial help while I'm looking for a job, and if I get approved, she says I can also ask for a clothing grant to get an outfit for interviews. Everything I owned was in a suitcase with Alec, so lord knows where that is now.

I make myself some toast and sit in the front room. I put the television on because some background noise helps me stay calm, and then I type out a text to Pit. I have no idea if he wants to hear from me anymore, but it makes me feel connected to someone.

Me: I don't even know if you have your mobile phone. Maybe you changed your number so you don't have to hear from me. But messaging you makes me somehow feel less alone in the world so for now, I'm going to keep updating you. Unless you tell me to stop. Today I met a man! Don't panic, he's a vicar . . . I think. He didn't wear the collar and the church wasn't some grand place of worship. He has a wife, she's really nice. They helped me look for a job and apply to the government for financial help while I get back on my feet. I really feel like this could be a fresh start. I miss you, Pit. x

PIT

I miss you, Pit. I stare at the last sentence and clench my jaw. She misses me . . . but she shouldn't. I am everything that's wrong in her life. She allows pricks like me in and then she thinks we're good for her. This is the reason I had to get away, because that kind of text would have had me straight back into her life. One text. That's all it would have taken for me to screw the rest of her life up.

My mobile rings in my hand and I answer, putting it to my ear. "Lucas," I greet.

"Just letting you know she turned up tonight."

"I know," I mutter, staring out over the water.

"She's nice. Damaged but nice."

I prickle at his words. "Damaged?"

"You're telling me she isn't?" he asks, and I hear him inhaling on a cigarette.

"Does Mary know you're still doing that shit?" I ask.

He sniggers. "You know, she reminded me of the women we used to watch on the estate."

I arch a brow. "The prostitutes?"

"We were just kids back then, we didn't know what they did for a living. But she has that same suspicious look in her eye, like she doesn't trust the world or anyone in it," he says.

"That's not a bad thing," I tell him. "Is she going for the interview?"

"I didn't want to make it look too obvious, so we went through the application process."

"Let me know when she takes it." I disconnect and release a long breath. I've known Lucas since we were five years old. We were on the same path—shit mothers, no education, and easy pickings for the local drug dealers to train up. We drifted when we turned eighteen, and he turned back up a year ago like a new man. He's got his life together with his wife and faith. The only thing the fucker does now is smoke. I sigh heavily, comparing my own life to his. I never wanted any of it before, until now . . . until her.

My phone beeps, and I open another text message from Tessa.

> Tessa: Is it weird if I sleep on the couch? I can't settle upstairs where I can't hear out for intruders. Plus, I like the television as background noise. Anyway, goodnight, Pit. I hope that wherever you are, you're okay. Miss you x

And there are those words again. It would be easy to type back. To tell her that, actually, I hate being this far away and even putting the sea between us isn't enough to stop me wanting her.

I want to reassure her that sleeping with the television on is just a coping mechanism, and that one day, she'll fall to sleep without it by accident and then she'll realise she doesn't need it anymore. I want to tell her that sleeping with the lights on doesn't stop the monsters, even if it makes her feel better, because monsters aren't afraid of the light or the dark. They'll come regardless, just like I did.

I cross the street and climb into the backseat of my next mark's car. He's too arrogant to check before he gets in after his quick session with his mistress, and he's too stupid to think the club wouldn't send someone to find him after he tipped the police off about our shipment movements. I get comfortable and check my watch, knowing his routine so well that when he steps into the street a second later, I smile to myself while wrapping a cord around my fists. *So fucking predictable.*

CHAPTER 17

TESSA

I pace outside the office, trying to calm my nerves. I check my watch for the hundredth time just as it strikes nine a.m.

A woman comes rushing over with her keys in one hand and a bag in the other. She looks harassed as she drops the bag and holds out her hand. "You must be Tessa?"

"Yes," I say, smiling as she shoves a key in the door and opens it. She grabs her bag and punches some numbers into a bleeping alarm, which immediately silences.

"I had a nightmare getting here," she huffs, dropping her bag again, this time by a desk. I close the door as she pulls up the blinds. "I hate London traffic. And could I find a place to park? No. Because as usual, the little shitbag who owns the vape shop three streets away nicked my space. Honestly, I'm ready to kill the fucker." I stare wide-eyed, and when I don't respond, she glances my way then winces. "Sorry. Shit, sorry." She waves her hand in the air dismissively. "I'm not a morning person, and I haven't had a coffee. Anita, by the way." She moves closer, holding out a hand, and I shake it.

"How about I make a coffee and you gather yourself?" I suggest. I point to a door behind her that states 'kitchen' on the label. "Through there?"

She smiles wide and gives a nod, shrugging from her jacket while I head that way. "Milk, no sugar," she tells me.

I manage to find my way around the small kitchen area easily and return minutes later with a hot coffee. Anita is in a small office at the back of the reception area with the door open. I pause in the doorway, and she glances up. "Come in," she tells me, and I place the coffee on her desk. "Thank you, you're a life saver. Please, take a seat."

I lower into the chair opposite her desk and cross my legs. The nerves seem to have calmed, and I suddenly feel proud of myself. *I've made it this far without a panic attack.*

"Okay, Tessa, I need someone who is literate enough to answer the telephone and take down messages I can read." She sips her coffee and closes her eyes for a brief second before adding, "And who makes a decent cuppa, so tick that box."

I smile. "I've been making coffee since I was six years old."

"You're hired," she says, and my eyes widen. "Seriously. I am that desperate, I'm hiring you for your coffee making skills."

I laugh nervously. "I can answer the telephone too."

"Perfect."

"And take messages."

"Even better. Any questions?"

"When can I start?"

"Exactly, when can you start?" she counters, and I laugh again.

"Now?"

She slams her hands on the desk. "Yes. Damn it, yes, I think I love you."

I release a breath and give a nod, pressing my lips together to hide my huge smile. "This is the salary and contract," she says, sliding an envelope toward me. "Temp for three months and then we'll assess. That's your desk," she adds, pointing to the reception desk. "The appointment book is in the drawer. We open at nine and take appointments from nine-thirty to three-thirty. I like to be out the door at five, earlier if possible."

"No problem." I stand. "Thanks so much, I really appreciate this."

"Keep the coffee coming and we'll get along just fine."

I pause at the door. "Erm, one more thing, what exactly do we do here?"

She laughs, throwing her head back. "You mean, Lucas didn't say?"

"Not exactly, just that it was an admin role."

"I'm a solicitor."

"Fantastic. I'll get settled."

I take a seat at the desk, placing my handbag underneath. I take a breath and release it slowly. I have a job. I smile to myself. *I did it, I have a bloody job!*

The telephone rings, startling me, and I jump before glancing back nervously at Anita. She gives an encouraging nod before saying, "Good morning, Jenson's Solicitors."

I give a nod and grab the telephone, repeating the sentence in a bright voice. "Anita?" a gruff voice barks on the other end.

"No, I'm Tessa, her new receptionist."

"Put her on," he snaps impatiently.

"Of course, can I take your name, please?"

"She left my bed an hour ago," he growls. "She knows who it is."

I press hold and turn back to Anita. "He's really cross," I tell her. "Wouldn't give a name but said you left his bed an hour ago."

She laughs again. "Was he rude?" I nod. "Then cut him off." I stare wide-eyed. "Seriously, just take him off hold and slam the phone down."

"Oh, I don't think that'll help his mood."

She grins. "Exactly." I do as she says, and a second later, it rings again. "If it's him and he's rude again, do the same. We don't speak to anyone who's rude. They all know the rules, including him."

I brace myself and answer, "Good morning, Jenson's Solicitors."

"Did you just fucking hang up on me?" he roars, and I wince before doing the same again. It's not how I've ever been instructed to deal with clients. When it rings again, I groan but answer regardless with the same bright tone.

"Please, can I talk to Anita?" he asks, and I can tell by his tone he's gritting his teeth in annoyance.

I smile, shocked her tactics work. "Of course, what name is it, please?"

"Atlas," he mutters.

"I'll just put you through."

I pop him on hold and turn to Anita, who's also smiling. "See, they soon remember. Press transfer and number one and that'll transfer him to me."

I do as she instructed, and she picks up the call. "Atlas," she greets. After a short pause, she says, "Your mood hasn't improved, I see." Then she gets up to close her office door.

∼

By lunchtime, I'm starting to relax. Anita explains everything so well and I feel like I'm picking everything up relatively easy. I even managed to have a quick glance over the contract and it seems good. The monthly wage is way more than I've ever earned and Anita's arranging for me to get paid weekly so I don't have to wait so long.

She points me in the direction of the nearest deli for lunch and gives me her bank card to pay on the provisor I grab her something too.

I pull out my mobile the second I'm out and call Pit, my smile soon fading when he still doesn't accept my call. Then I grab some lunch and sit on a metal bench across the road. I open the texts I've already sent him.

> Me: Guess what, I got a job! The woman is amazing. She's crazy and doesn't take any shit. I think she'll be good for me, Pit. She's already working on toughening me up. I just wanted you to know I'm doing good. I miss you x

I head back to the office feeling slightly less happy. Sharing my exciting news with Pit in a one-way text message doesn't feel as good.

PIT

"Anita," I greet. "How's she doing?"

"Great. Honestly, Pit, I feel like you did me the favour, not the other way around. Where did you find such a gem?"

I prop my feet up on the desk, ignoring the man I have tied to a wooden stool opposite me who's struggling to break free with a wild panic in his eyes.

"She's one in a million."

"She sure is. I even had her hang up on Atlas today for being rude."

I pull my feet back to the floor and sit straighter. "Rude how?" I demand.

She laughs. "Relax, he was just blunt, but I could tell she needed to feel more in control. I can't have the boys walking all over her now, can I?"

The thought pisses me off, but I take a calming breath. "Just watch her for me, Nita. I don't want her upset. She's been through a lot."

"And I assume that's to do with you?"

"Just make sure everyone is respectful." I disconnect and tuck my phone away. "Women," I utter, shaking my head. "Why do we worry so much?"

The man groans into his gag, and I step around the desk, resting my backside against the edge and taking a screwdriver from my inside pocket. "I just happened to be in the area and Steven dropped your name, so I thought I should pay you a visit."

He moans into the gag some more, and I roll my eyes before leaning closer and ripping the sticky tape away. He winces. "Man, I haven't seen Stevo for years."

"You were good friends though back in the day, right?" I'd searched Steven Kendal's social media messages to get me to this point. The ones to this fucker stood out the most, where they were catching up just a year ago and laughing about the time they locked Tessa in the music cupboard and she'd pissed herself with fright. Maybe his story rang too close to the way she'd reacted when I'd done similar. Maybe the guilt was too much. But here we are, and as I look into the cruel eyes of Lee Hive, I absolutely have no intention of walking away.

"Yeah, but we were kids back then."

I hold my hand up, cutting him off. "See, you already know this isn't going to be good because you're trying to make up excuses. I'm gonna say a name, and you're going to tell me your part in her life." He eyes me warily. "Tessa."

He shakes his head frantically, "I don't know no Tessa."

"Tessa Dean."

I see the realisation hit him, followed quickly by confusion. "I haven't seen her in years."

"Tell me about the last time you saw her," I suggest, folding my arms over my chest and fixing him with an expectant glare.

He shrugs. "Fuck, I don't remember. We were kids."

"Think," I push.

"Maybe year eleven."

"That was around the time Steven began dating her, right?"

He smirks. "Is that what this is about? Are you some new boyfriend who's jealous of her exes?"

"It would be simple for you if that was my reason," I tell him, unfolding my arms. I spin the screwdriver between my fingers, circling him. He tracks me with his eyes until I move behind him, then I lean over his shoulder and slam the pointy end into his thigh. He cries out immediately, and I shove a cloth in his mouth to muffle his screams. "When I heard you were in Ireland, I thought it was fate," I whisper, smiling. "Now, think carefully, Lee. What happened to Tessa back in school?" I pull the cloth from his mouth.

"Jesus," he cries, "ow the fuck can I remember almost twenty years ago?"

I pull out Steven's mobile phone and open the messages between them. "Music room?" I ask.

He sags, the fight leaving him. "I was a stupid teenager."

"Very stupid," I agree. "And I did some digging into your life, Lee. The things I saw were not good."

"Who the fuck are you?"

"I'm the reason you'll never bully anyone ever again," I confirm, driving the screwdriver into his opposite leg. He cries out again, but this time, I punch him hard in the face, busting his nose and knocking out a tooth. "You've had several complaints at work, all women saying a similar thing—you make inappropriate comments, give unwanted attention, touching at every opportunity."

"They were ganging up on me," he yells, spitting blood onto the floor.

"All of them?" I ask, laughing coldly. "I couldn't work out how you always seem to get away with it, and then I realised you went to school with your boss."

"Look, I'm sorry I made Tessa upset, okay," he shouts. "But she was a whining little bitch, thinking she was better than everyone else. We all knew her dad was a drunk who beat her mum."

I punch him in the face again, and he curses, shaking his head. "So, you knew she was already having a shit time and you bullied her anyway? Scum."

"She was scum," he spits. "Even her dad hated her."

"What are you talking about?"

"He paid Steven to date her. He wanted her out the house as much as possible cos she reminded him of his wife."

I allow his words to sink in. "Is he still alive?"

"Her dad?" He nods. "Yeah, he's alive."

"Where?"

He scoffs. "Let me go and I'll tell you."

I hit him a third time, following it quickly with a punch to his stomach. He leans forward, coughing violently. "I'm in charge. I want the address, and then I'll consider letting you leave."

He gives a stiff nod, and I grab a piece of paper and a pen. "Shoot," I say, and he reels off a street name.

"It's in Cardiff. He drinks with my uncle. I don't know the house number, but someone round there will know him."

I stand, shaking out my shoulders. "No one will miss

you, Lee," I say with a shrug, "and that's so sad." Before he can say anything else, I push the screwdriver into his neck. His eyes widen in surprise, and he begins to cough, spilling blood down his chin. I withdraw it, wiping the end on his jeans before heading out. I close the office door and rush down the metal steps, heading out the factory and into the dark night.

I check my mobile and see another text.

> Tessa: Still can't sleep in the bed. Luckily the couch is comfy. Goodnight, Pit. Miss you x

I smile. *I miss you too, Te.*

CHAPTER 18

TESSA

"It's Friday, and it's tradition," Anita says.

I smile as she rests her hands on my desk and stares down at me with hopeful eyes. "I'm just not really a drinker," I tell her with a shrug.

"Bullshit. It's your second full week and you've done amazing. You refused to let me celebrate last Friday, so we're doing this." She grabs my hand, and I snatch my bag from the floor. "And you look amazing in that dress, it's a shame not to show it off."

I straighten the tight, fitted dress I got in a sale last weekend with my first pay cheque. I also managed to get some office wear from a charity shop which saved me looking unprofessional this week. "Bars make me nervous," I add as she drags me towards the door.

"I'll look after you."

"And men make me uncomfortable."

She pauses and glances back at me. "Oh shit, Te, are you a lesbian? I didn't realise."

"No," I rush to say.

"It's fine, I'm not against it or anything," she tells me, locking up the office.

"I'm not a lesbian," I argue, and a passing couple snigger. I feel my face burning with embarrassment as Anita hooks her arm through mine.

"Look, Te, I've spent a fortnight analysing you and it doesn't take a genius to see that social situations make you uncomfortable. But I promise to break you in gently. I won't leave your side, and if you hate it after twenty minutes, you can leave." I groan out loud, and she smirks. "Thanks."

She leads me to a bar a few doors down from the office, telling me lots of office types drink here on a Friday. It's not too busy, which makes me relax slightly, and Anita orders us each a drink, taking the pressure off me to choose, because I have no idea what tastes good when it comes to cocktails.

We take fruity-looking red drinks over to a table by the window, and she eases from her jacket and hangs it on the back of her chair. "So, how was your second week?"

"Good," I reply, nodding. I love working with her—she's lively and funny, and she doesn't make me feel different. "I'm really enjoying it."

"I know I've said it a million times already, but I don't know what I did without you. Your filing system is perfect. I can find every file."

"It's a standard system," I say with a laugh. "Your desk pile wasn't."

She laughs too. "You're right. I have zero organisational skills." I take a sip from the drink, and when my eyes light up, she grins. "Good, right?"

"This is amazing," I whisper, taking another sip.

"You deserve it after all your hard work." She leans a little closer. "So, Tessa, spill . . . are you married, single, or other?"

"Well, I'd like to repeat I am not a lesbian." She laughs harder. "But I am single. Very much single."

"Me too."

"What about the guy who keeps ringing . . . Atlas?"

"God, no, we're just sleeping together." I almost choke on the drink and grab a napkin to wipe my chin. "He's . . . how do I put it? Possessive . . . angry . . . annoying."

"So, why are you sleeping with him?"

"Because the guy is a genius in the bedroom." We both giggle like teenagers, and I drink some more. A waiter passes, and Anita orders another round. "Have you ever met a guy who makes you light up in the bedroom and knows exactly what to do?" she asks, fanning her face with a beer mat.

I picture Pit and smile. "Yeah."

"Now, that is a look of love," she comments, arching a brow.

I shake my head. "Nothing like that. It was a short fling . . . I think. Anyway, he's gone, so it doesn't matter anymore."

"You miss him," she guesses.

"He doesn't miss me, and that's what really matters."

"Well, it's his loss," she says, clinking her glass against mine, and we finish off the cocktails just as new ones are placed down.

I'M NOT sure what number cocktail we're on anymore, but my head is fuzzy and I'm suddenly extremely tired. I rest my head against the cubicle wall while I pee. I close my eyes and think about Pit again. Why the hell can't I get him out of my head?

> Me: I miss you. Why won't you text me, Pit? I'm in a bar, drunk. That's a first. Another first. But this one is without you, again. I hate that.

When I return to Anita, two men have joined the table. I hesitate, but she spots me and waves me over.

I slide into my seat and offer an awkward smile. It's not like they're bad looking, in fact, they're both seriously good looking and dressed well. "This is my friend, Tessa," Anita tells them, and I blush harder. *She called me her friend, not her employee.*

"Te, this is Mark and Will. They work as barristers, and we sometimes send work their way."

I relax knowing they're more like colleagues than potential dates. "Great to meet you," I say, sipping my drink.

"I was filling them in on Mister Sky," she adds, and we both laugh. The client came in this week needing representation for stealing ten vibrators from a well-known high-street store.

While they get lost in conversation, I check my phone. There's nothing, and my heart feels heavy as I tuck my phone away.

"Waiting for him to call?" asks Mark, leaning closer.

I force a smile. "No, just checking my messages."

"So, there's no one special?"

Anita's mobile rings and she rolls her eyes, cancelling the call. I smirk, knowing full well it's the mysterious Atlas.

"I'm not looking for anything," I reply.

"Hey, neither am I," he replies, holding up his hands in defence. "But I don't want some guy coming in here assuming the worst and punching my lights out."

I laugh. "That won't happen."

Somehow, we move onto shots. One shot for every time Will mentions his ex's name, which seems often since they've not long split up and he's cut up.

The room is spinning, and I'm definitely going to regret this by the morning.

PIT

I pace, staring at the text message I received from Tessa over an hour ago. My mobile lights up in my hand and I answer. "Atlas, what the fuck's going on?" I demand.

"I've tried calling Nita, brother, but she's ignoring me."

"Don't you track her?"

"No, she'd rip my balls off. We respect each other's space."

"Fuck that. Find them."

"Aww shit," I hear him mutter.

"What?"

"She sent me a pic."

"So?"

"She's with a guy."

"What guy?" I yell. "Where's Tessa?"

"With them."

"Send me the picture," I grit out.

It comes through a second later, and I stare hard at Tessa's smiling face as some guy tucks her into his side. My heart slams harder, twisting with each beat. "It's the cocktail bar near her office," I mutter. "I'll meet you there."

I landed back in London at five this morning and haven't slept in over twenty-four hours. But as my bike rolls to a stop outside the wine bar, I feel wide awake.

Atlas fist bumps me. "They're still inside," he says.

I pull my cap down over my eyes and my hood over it. "Let's go."

Inside, it's quiet, with most people moving on for either food or a night club. I hear her before I see her, and it takes me by surprise because she's usually so quiet. I peer up from under my cap and see her with her head thrown back and a laugh escaping, and I find myself smiling. Then, suddenly, she sits up straight and covers her mouth, her eyes filled with panic. She dives up out her chair and rushes past me and outside.

Anita stands in alarm, then her eyes land on us and she groans. "What the fuck are you doing here?"

"You didn't answer my call," snaps Atlas.

"Because you're not my keeper," she shouts.

I head out after Tessa, not bothering to stick around to listen to the domestic unfolding.

Tessa is on her knees with her head stuck in a bush. The doorman smirks as I move closer to her and gently run a hand over her back.

"Sorry," she mumbles. "I just need a—" The sound of retching ensues.

I wait for it to stop and for her to back out the bush before scooping her into my arms and flagging down a cab. She rests her head against my chest, not bothering to open her eyes as I climb into the back seat, keeping her on my knee.

The cab stops outside her place a few minutes later, and I carry her to the door, searching my pocket for my keys to let us in. I turn off the alarm and take her straight up to bed, laying her in the centre, where she immediately curls into a ball. I remove her shoes and drag a thick blanket over her. Then I turn on the lamp beside the bed and take a seat in the armchair, watching her sleep, seething that she has no idea where she is or how she got here. I could have been anyone.

~

I MUST NOD off because I wake with a start, looking around frantically and relaxing when my eyes land on Tessa's sleeping form. It's light outside.

Heading downstairs, I take her phone with me. I open the pictures, skipping through the ones she took last night of her and Anita, then both of them with the two guys, then one of her and one of the guys. I scowl, deleting the pictures. Then I open the contacts, where I see my number, Anita's, the office, and then Mark. *Mark.* I hate him already. I block the number and then delete it.

I take a bottle of water back upstairs with a couple paracetamol and set them on the bedside cabinet. Then I gently press my lips to her forehead. She stirs, mumbling my name as I back out the room, head downstairs, and out the door, dropping the latch as I leave.

∽

I PICK my bike up from outside the bar and head to the clubhouse. Axel is in his office, and he stands when I head in, shaking my hand. "You weren't gone long."

"I have some shit to deal with here," I tell him. "I was gonna call, but the flight was last minute and early."

"Everything okay?"

I nod, and we take a seat. "I'm back for Tessa's dad."

He arches a brow. "Brother, you're cleaning up all these loose ends for her, why the fuck don't you claim her?"

I shake my head. "She needs a different life."

"Have you asked her?"

"No, and I don't intend to. Pres, I treated her like shit."

"But she's forgiven you. If she hadn't, she wouldn't be leaving you messages."

"She's too traumatised to make those kinds of decisions."

"So, you're going to wipe out every fucker who ever did anything to add to her trauma?"

"Something like that."

"Are you gonna top yourself at the end of it?" asks Grizz, entering the office. "Cos you're on the list too."

Axel sniggers. "Look, do what you gotta do and then go and speak to her. She should at least know everything you've done for her."

"No," I say firmly. "She can't ever know about the job or the loose ends. I don't want her pretty little head filled with shit I've done. She just needs to move on and meet a nice guy," I say.

They exchange a doubtful look. "But when she meets someone, you're gonna turn up and pull her out of there?" asks Grizz, and I realise Atlas has told them about last night.

"He wasn't right for her," I snap.

Axel grins. "You'll feel like that about them all, brother, trust me."

I push to my feet. "I need to go check out her dad's place. Can I take Atlas with me?"

Axel nods. "Sure. He needs to clear his head with all this shit around Anita."

I head upstairs and push Atlas's door open. He sits up, his eyes shooting open, relaxing when he sees it's me. "Fuck, brother, I thought it was another police raid."

Anita stirs beside him, stretching out and opening one eye. "You joining us, Pit?" she asks with a smirk, and Atlas shakes his head in annoyance, muttering under his breath.

"Get up," I tell him. "We're riding out in ten."

"To?"

"Cardiff."

"Any particular reason?" he asks, throwing his legs over the side of the bed and tugging his jeans on.

"Unfinished business."

"For Tessa?" he asks, arching a brow.

Anita sits up. "Is she okay? She was pretty wasted last night."

"No thanks to you," I say dryly.

"You asked me to look after her, and she needed to loosen up a bit."

I narrow my eyes. "She's fine the way she is," I snap.

Anita smiles. "I know that, but she craves to live the sort of life that she sees every other woman her age living. Drinks with the girls, dinner dates, and movie nights with a lover."

"What lover?" I spit, clenching my fists into tight balls.

"She's not going to be single forever, Pit. The girl wants company."

"Did she say that?"

"Not exactly."

"Then don't be encouraging it," I warn. "I asked you to employ her, not get her laid."

"She's got needs . . ." Anita begins, but Atlas cuts her off with a warning glare, sensing I'm ready to explode, and she presses her lips together in a fine line.

"And if she asks, I wasn't there last night. As far as she's concerned, I'm still across the water."

"She must have seen you," she says.

"Like you pointed out, she was wasted and immediately fell asleep. Another reason you shouldn't get her into that state, anyone could've taken her and she wouldn't have had a fucking clue."

"Jesus, Pit, claim her already," she mutters, flopping back and pulling the sheets over herself.

CHAPTER 19

TESSA

I'm already at my desk when Anita arrives wearing over-sized shades. I smirk as she passes my desk muttering, "Good morning."

I go into the kitchenette and make her a coffee, also grabbing the pastry I picked up for her on the way in this morning. She's got her head in her hands when I place the items on her desk, and she glances up, removing her shades. "I am too old to spend the weekend drinking like I'm nineteen," she murmurs.

I laugh. "Yeah, I won't be making a habit of repeating Friday night again. Why do people drink like that?"

She frowns. "You've never been drunk before?"

"Of course, just nothing like that. I have very vague memories of the night. I don't even remember getting home, but I woke fully dressed and somehow remembered to get myself a bottle of water and paracetamol."

"Weird," she says, a strange look passing over her face.

"And I swear I saw my . . . ex." I give my head a shake. "Well, not my ex, just a . . . never mind, I don't know what he was. Either way, I really thought he'd taken me home." I laugh to myself. "Wishful thinking."

I head back to my desk just as the door opens and a large biker fills the doorway, one I recognise from the club Pit belongs to. My heart immediately speeds up, and I force myself to smile. I know he isn't here for me—*why would he be*—but seeing that logo on his jacket sets some kind of alarm off inside me, making me want to run in the opposite direction.

"Do you have an appointment?" I ask, my voice wavering slightly.

"She's expecting me," he mutters, looking past me to Anita.

"You don't have an appointment, Kade," she shouts from her office.

"Atlas sent me," he replies.

"Jesus," she says to herself. "It's fucking Monday morning. I don't have the time or patience for this shit."

"Don't shoot the messenger," he argues.

He heads into her office, and she closes the door. Meanwhile, my heart races faster. She knows The Chaos Demons, and it sounds like Atlas is one of them.

Minutes later, Kade storms from the office, pulling out his mobile as he leaves. Anita leans on the doorframe of her office and sighs loudly. "That fucker tries way too hard to control me," she says out loud.

I turn to face her. "You know The Chaos Demons?"

She glances down with a guilty expression. "Uh-huh."

"So, you know Pit?" She finally meets my eyes and gives a nod. My heart races. "Was he there on Friday?" I hold my breath, waiting for her answer. Eventually, she gives a slight nod. "Was it coincidence he was there?"

"No."

I eye her suspiciously. "And did he take me home?"

"Yes."

"But he didn't want me to know?" She gives her head a shake. "Why?"

Anita lets out a long breath. "I have no idea, Tessa. He's in turmoil over you, like he can't bear to see you with anyone else, but he's keeping his distance."

I briefly close my eyes, thinking back to that night. I knew it was him the second I felt a hand on my back. The way he scooped me into his arms, and how his scent filled my nostrils, it instantly calmed me.

"I thought I was imagining him," I say, narrowing my eyes. "So, this job . . ."

She holds up her hands, already shaking her head. "I employed you because I liked you and you're bloody good at the job."

"But before that, did he set this up?"

She groans. "Look, he doesn't want you to know all this, Tessa. And if I tell you, he's going to be annoyed with me, and honestly, it's a stress I can do without."

"How did you meet Atlas?" I ask, changing the subject. Maybe talking about herself might ease the tension.

"How about we go for dinner after work and I'll tell you?" I give a nod, and she smiles before heading back into her office.

I'M nervous as we enter the restaurant. All I've thought about all day is Pit and how far he's gone to make sure I'm okay. And I have a thousand unanswered questions, like has he done all this because of guilt or because deep down he likes me?

WE'RE SEATED and given menus. I stare at the prices and bite my lower lip with worry. As if sensing my unease, Anita places her hand over mine and offers a reassuring smile. "Relax, it's on the business. We'll call it a meeting. Order whatever you want."

"Do you get a lot of work from the club?" I ask, and she laughs out loud.

"Yes. I handle most of their legal work these days."

We fall silent, studying the menu, and when the waiter returns with two glasses of wine, we each order a steak and salad.

I take a sip of the sweet white. "So, you and Atlas?"

"Me and Atlas," she repeats, sighing heavily. "We hook up."

"He seems way more into it than that."

"Yeah, well, I try to break it off when he gets too much, but somehow, he always convinces me to stick around."

"You don't want a relationship?" I ask.

The waiter places some bread and olives between us. Anita pops one into her mouth before taking a chunk of bread and dipping it into the oils. "I like being free."

"He does seem quite grumpy."

She smirks. "That's one of the reasons I love . . . like him," she says, blushing slightly at her error.

"So, if you *like* him so much, what's the problem?"

"What about you and Pit?" she asks, ignoring my question. "How did you guys meet?"

It's my turn to laugh. "I was in the wrong place at the wrong time," I say vaguely. I'm not sure if Anita knows the ways of the club or if she'd understand our situation.

"So, it wasn't love at first sight?" I shake my head. "And now, he's avoiding you?"

I groan. "Don't remind me. He just left one day, and I wasn't expecting it."

"But now, he's back," she says with a shrug.

"Clearly not for me."

"Maybe you should take the choice away from him," she suggests.

I take some of the bread. "What do you mean?"

"He's into you, Tessa, but for whatever reason, he's holding back in the shadows. If he's anything like Atlas, he'll make sure you never meet anyone else."

"I don't think he cares," I admit. "I met the guys on Friday, right?"

"And he showed up and took you home," she points out. "Mark gave you his number, do you still have it?"

I frown and take out my phone, opening the contacts. "No," I say. "Are you sure he gave it to me?"

She nods. "I handed him your phone myself. Pit deleted it."

"He wouldn't," I mutter.

"What about the pictures you took with Mark, are they still there?" I open my pictures and shake my head. I don't remember taking pictures either, but Anita seems certain. "I put a picture of us all on my social media, and within twenty minutes, Atlas and Pit showed up. It wasn't a coincidence, Te. And if he didn't like you so much, why would he care enough to make sure he erases your pictures so you don't recall Mark and deletes the number so you can't contact him? He cockblocked you."

I try to hide my smile, but it breaks through. I'm glad he did. I wouldn't have called Mark anyway or hooked up with him. "I've been texting Pit every day. He never replies."

"So, text him now and tell him you know everything. He'll soon come running, and if he doesn't, tell him you're meeting up with Mark despite his attempt to sabotage you. That'll definitely get his attention."

PIT

"We've been watching this shithole for the last twelve hours. He clearly isn't here," Atlas complains.

We'd knocked on several doors at the top of the street before we were pointed in the direction of Greg Dean's house. The elderly lady who gave him up insisted we have tea and cake with her, much to Atlas's annoyance, but it paid off because she told us all kinds of stuff about her annoying neighbour. She definitely didn't hold back.

"Maybe someone tipped him off," I suggest.

I start my bike up just as the elderly neighbour rushes over holding a piece of paper. "Mister Daykin from around the corner just spotted him going into the local pub," she yells over the engine. I take the paper and smile.

"You're a legend," I tell her. "Thanks."

The pub is just around the corner. We dismount and head inside. "Two whiskeys," I tell the barman, who eyes our kuttes warily.

I glance around the empty bar. There're only two men in the entire place, and one of those is far too young to be Tessa's father. We take our drinks and head over to the older man. It's obvious the years haven't been kind to him as he drags his eyes up to watch as we take a seat opposite him. "We've been looking for you," I tell him.

He stares at the badge on my kutte. "Pit," he says, like the word leaves a bad taste in his mouth. "I don't owe nothing. I cleared all my debt."

"Greg, right?" I ask.

He sneers. "Well, son, if you aren't sure of my name, I certainly ain't gonna tell yah."

"Greg," calls the barman, and he groans, "don't forget to clear your tab before you leave or the boss will string me up."

I smirk. "Let me get that for you." I head back to the bar, pulling out my wallet. "What's he owe?"

"A tonne," he tells me, and I give a low whistle while I count the notes out and lay them on the bar. "For a week," he adds, shaking his head with disappointment.

"It's clear he's got a problem," I mutter. "Why do you keep serving him?"

"He goes way back with the landlord. Besides, when we refuse, he gets all aggressive, and we can't be arsed with the fight. Why you paying it anyway? Do you know him?"

I shake my head. "No." I place another two hundred on the bar. "What's the CCTV like in here?"

He glances around nervously. "It's not working."

"Is that for real, or are you lying to me?"

"For real. The boss don't like eyes everywhere. He's not exactly law abiding."

I slide the money closer. "We were never here, right?"

He scoops it. "My lips are sealed."

I head back over to the table. "One hundred, cleared."

"Who the fuck are you?" Greg spits.

"We're gonna go for a little walk," I say. "Get up."

"No fucking way," he snaps. "What do you want?"

"I have a message from Tessa," I say, heading for the door. "Bring him," I tell Atlas.

Seconds later, we're standing outside with Atlas gripping Greg's upper arm tightly. He steers him back towards his house.

Greg reluctantly unlocks the front door and the smell of shit hits us immediately. "What the hell is that?" asks Atlas, pulling his shirt up over his nose and shoving Greg into the house.

I do the same as we head inside. The place is a mess with refuse discarded carelessly on the floor amongst dog faeces. An elderly-looking pit bull stands when we enter the living room, and I give his head a stroke. He closes his eyes and nuzzles against me. He's underweight and covered in sores. "This dog needs to see a vet," I snap.

"I don't have the money for that," he replies, flopping into an armchair. "He's on his last legs anyway. So, what's that miserable cow have to say?"

"Do you remember Steven Kendal?" I ask, putting a

cigarette in my mouth and lighting it. He watches me longingly.

"No."

I hold out the lit cigarette to him, and he goes to take it, but I pull it out of reach. "Think."

"The kid Tessa dated?"

"The kid you paid to date her," I correct.

He smiles, nodding. "That's right. She needed a good fuck to lighten up. Apparently, she was hard work and he got sick of her."

"Do you know he bullied her for years?"

"What's this all got to do with me?" Greg asks impatiently.

I take a long drag on the cigarette and slowly release the smoke into the air. "Cos when she told me about it, I got pissed."

"So?"

"And when I get pissed, I do stupid shit."

"Like turn up to her dad's place to whine?" he asks, smirking.

I pull out my blade and slam it into his chest without missing a beat. His eyes widen, and I lean in close to his ear. "No, like kill people," I whisper.

"Christ, Pit. A warning would've been nice," mutters Atlas.

"What's up, the sight of blood make you sick?" I ask with a grin. I withdraw the knife, and Greg grabs my wrist, trying to push me away as I drive it in a second time, straight into his cold heart. "Rest in hell, you sick fucker."

I clean my knife on his trousers and stick it back in my

inside pocket. The dog is watching me with his big eyes, and I groan. "I'm on a bike," I tell him like he understands.

"We can't take that thing back," snaps Atlas.

"I can't leave it."

"He'll probably eat the guy's body and thrive," he says with a laugh.

"I can't let him eat that disgusting fucker. He's coming with us."

"How?"

"I'll sit him between my legs. We'll just have to keep stopping for breaks."

"Great," he mutters, rolling his eyes. "All this shit for a woman you ain't even claiming."

"This was my redemption for what I did to her," I admit, scooping the dog into my arms because he appears too weak to walk far.

"Let's hope she wasn't too attached to her dad," he mutters, following me out.

CHAPTER 20

TESSA

I stare at the message I've typed out, my finger hovering over the send button. I take a deep breath and hit it.

> Me: I know everything, Pit. You brought me home Friday. You got me the job with Anita. Do not ignore me this time. I want to see you.

I keep the phone in my hand and wait for the reply. After five minutes, I realise it's not coming, and that just hurts my heart some more.

I open my social media app and scroll through. I don't use it really, only to see how amazing everyone else's life is, but it's not like I have many friends. Anita forced me to add her earlier, and I have some old school nerds on there, the ones who let me hang around with them. Most were too scared of getting Steven's attention, so they often avoided me too.

I stare at a picture shared by one of the girls who'd

allowed me to eat lunch at her table. The caption reads, *'So sad to hear the news about Lee Hive who was found dead. RIP.'* Lee was a good friend of Steven's, and even though I know it's almost impossible, I wonder if it's a coincidence he's now dead too.

I'm too scared to search his name, in case this somehow leads back to me, and I shut my phone off. I'm being ridiculous.

I lie down on the couch and close my eyes. I was amazed when I woke in my bed. I even texted Pit that morning, telling him I'd made it a night in the actual bedroom. I feel stupid now, knowing that he already knew, and I groan out loud. Since then, I've gone back to sleeping on the couch. There's something about being closer to the door that settles me.

I wake with a start and realise the room is in darkness. I must have fallen to sleep. I reach around for my mobile, pulling it closer to check the time. There's still no reply from Pit, and my heart sinks.

I push to sit up and the lamp turns on, making me jump. Pit is sitting in the armchair, his face stern. "You're here," I whisper.

"What exactly do you think you know?" he asks.

His voice sends shivers down my spine, and that spark of nerves builds in my stomach. "You were with me on Friday."

"Yes."

"And you know Anita. You got me the job, which means you probably know Lucas."

"Yes."

"Why?"

"Redemption," he mutters.

I bite my lower lip, mulling over my next question. "Lee Hive is dead," I blurt out, and he keeps his face neutral. "Do you know about that?"

"Yes."

I inhale sharply. "But how did you know about him?"

"Your dad is also dead," he says bluntly.

My eyebrows shoot up in surprise. "What?"

"He paid Steven Kendal to date you, Te. He wanted you out the way. He paid him, knowing he was bullying you."

I stare open-mouthed, though not because I'm shocked at learning that new information. My dad was a pig, so it doesn't surprise me. But the fact Pit has been on a rampage . . . for me.

"Do you see now," he continues, "why I'm not good enough for you?"

"You did all that for me," I whisper.

"Because I'm fucked-up, Te. I'm not normal."

"But you did that for me," I repeat, standing and moving towards him. I notice his hands tighten their hold on the arms of the chair as he watches me cautiously. "No one's ever done that sort of thing for me." I gently place my hands on his cheeks. "Thank you." I kiss him. It's bold and so unlike me, but the urge to go to him, to show him how grateful I am, is too overwhelming to ignore. He's frozen, but as my tongue sweeps into his mouth, I feel him relax. And then his hands slide up my waist and he pulls me into his lap, kissing me back with just as much passion.

A whining sound makes us pull apart. My lips feel swollen, and my heart is beating wildly in my chest. I glance around, my eyes landing on the emaciated dog cowering beside the armchair, wrapped in a towel. "What is that?" I whisper.

"A present," he tells me, smiling.

"It's a dog. A sick-looking dog," I add, frowning.

"Yeah. He needs some TLC."

"And a bath."

I climb from his lap and drop to my knees, holding out my hand for the dog to sniff. He does so cautiously. "He was with your dad," Pit adds.

I stroke the dog's bony head. "He mistreated you too," I mutter, and the dog leans into my touch. He drags himself closer until he can rest his head in my lap, and my heart melts a little.

"Maybe you can learn to trust together," Pit suggests.

"I told you, I'm scared of big dogs," I remind him. Pit stands, reaching down to scoop the dog into his arms. The thought of him taking him away makes me stand too. "But I guess I can see how it goes," I rush to add.

Pit grins. "I wasn't taking him away. I don't know if King and Gigi will take to a new dog, and this guy needs someone to care for him. I know you can do it, Te."

"What's his name?" I ask, following Pit up the stairs.

"Whatever you want it to be."

"Hope?" I suggest, and Pit laughs.

"You can't call him that. He'll get bullied by other big dogs if you call that out in the park."

I grin as we go into the bathroom. "Lucky?"

"That's a cat's name."

"You said whatever I want," I argue. "What about Chance?"

Pit gives a nod. "Chance, it is."

He dumps the dog in the bath and turns on the shower, making sure it's pointed away while he waits for the temperature to get warmer. He shrugs out of his kutte, handing it to me, and I place it on the hook at the back of the door. "Did he say anything?" I ask, watching as his tattooed hands run through Chance's fur.

"Your dad?" I nod. "No. I didn't give him a chance. But he's still a prick. The neighbours hate him. He takes prostitutes in, and they steal from the locals. He owes money all over the place and his house was a shithole. The dog crapped everywhere, and he didn't clean it up. There was no food in for the poor thing," he tells me, taking my shampoo from the shelf and squirting it over Chance. He massages it in, taking his time.

"Do you have to leave again?" I ask, holding my breath for his answer.

"It depends," he says, rinsing the shampoo away, "on whether you want me to leave."

I turn away to grab a towel, smiling to myself. "Do you want to stay?" I ask, handing it to him.

He wraps Chance up and lifts him from the tub, passing him to me. He's lighter than I expected, and I take him back downstairs, where I set him on the kitchen floor and begin to rub him dry.

Pit joins us with the quilt cover from the spare bed. "He can sleep on this," he says, placing it in the corner of the kitchen floor. "I'll pick him a bed up when the shops open."

He goes to my fridge and pulls out a pack of ham.

Kneeling beside me, he breaks pieces off and handfeeds them to Chance, who gobbles them greedily.

"Poor thing," I mutter, tickling him under the chin.

"It's a new start," says Pit. "For both of you."

"And you?" I ask.

His smile fades. "You don't know what you're getting into."

I stop drying Chance and turn to him. "Why are you fighting this?"

"Because I need you to know what you're agreeing too, Tessa." He gives the dog the rest of the ham and stands. I follow, waiting patiently while he washes his hands. Chance curls up on the quilt and closes his eyes. "He's made himself at home," says Pit with a smile.

I follow him into the living room, and he sits down, pulling me to join him on the couch. "I've never done this before," he admits. "I've never wanted to. But I can't stop thinking about you."

"Same."

"I thought space would make you realise I was no good. That maybe your feelings were down to being held captive. But you kept texting me and sharing your good days with me, and it made me realise I want to be a part of those days too."

"I want that too," I agree.

"You say that now," he says, guiding my legs to rest over his and placing his hand over my knee, "but I'll be unbearably suffocating, Te. I don't know how to be anything else. I'm jealous and possessive. A walking red flag."

"In case you didn't know, I tend to ignore red flags," I say with a small laugh.

"Which is why I'm doing the rational thinking for us both. I mean, what the fuck would we tell people when they ask how we met?"

"It's none of their business?" I suggest.

He groans, letting his head fall back against the couch so he's staring at the ceiling. "Help me out here, Tessa. Give me the reasons to walk away. I mean, fuck, I've killed people."

I mull over his words. He killed them for me. It's extreme, crazy even, but the way I feel for him outweighs everything else. My heart aches. I don't want him to walk away again. "Because I think I love you," I almost whisper. His head shoots upright, and he stares at me wide-eyed. I instantly regret it and bury my face in my hands. "Oh god, it's too soon, isn't it? Sorry. I'm rushing ahead of myself."

He tugs my hands away. "Say it again."

I swallow the lump in my throat and stare him in the eyes. I'm embarrassed, but the fire in his gaze burns brighter, so I repeat it. "I love you."

He inhales sharply as a range of emotions pass over his face. Then he surprises me by pulling me onto his lap so I'm sitting over him. "Again," he whispers, cupping my face in his hands.

"I love you."

He presses his lips to mine, his mouth slowly working wonders as he kisses me until my toes curl. When he finally pulls back slightly, he says, "I love you too."

I gasp. "You do?" He nods, and relief floods me. I kiss him again, and I feel his erection pressing against me.

"Sorry," he mutters when we break apart again.

"It's fine," I reassure him, but he looks away like he's ashamed.

"Go upstairs and get into bed. I'll check on Chance and be up shortly."

"You're staying?" I ask, smiling.

"We're never gonna be apart again," he tells me, stroking his hand down my cheek.

PIT

I wake with a start and stare into the eyes of Chance. His tongue darts out, and he licks my nose. I groan, rolling onto my back. "Tessa, why is there a dog between us?" I murmur sleepily.

Her head pops up over Chance, and she smiles. "Good morning."

"The dog?" I ask again.

She giggles, climbing over the dog and lying over me with her legs either side of mine. We'd done well last night to sleep in the same bed and not touch. She's not ready for that, and I insisted she wear full pyjamas while I remained in my jeans and T-shirt. But now, as she presses against me, I'm struggling to control my cock as it rises between us. "Tessa," I mutter in warning.

She looks up innocently. "It's just a cuddle," she says, smirking.

"You're not ready," I remind her.

"How do you know?" she argues. It's the same thing

she said last night as I held her in my arms until she'd fallen to sleep.

"I just know." She sighs heavily, and I smile to myself, tracing my fingers up and down her back. "We need to go see Axel today."

"Why?"

"Because he's my President and he's the first person I need to talk to about us."

"What if he says you can't stay?"

"We'll cross that bridge," I mutter. Axel has other brothers who would jump at the chance to live life on the road, so I don't think it'll be a huge problem. But with Axel, you never know what he's thinking.

WE GET to the clubhouse an hour later and head straight for the office. Tessa squeezes my hand, and I give her a reassuring smile. I want her to feel comfortable here at the club, but I know it'll take time.

Axel looks up as we enter and frowns, his eyes falling to our joined hands. He chucks his pen down on the desk and leans back in his chair. "This is the part where you tell me you wanna stick around," he guesses.

"I'd like to, Pres," I say firmly.

"You'd better take a seat," he mutters, and we sit down. "Are you gonna stay at the clubhouse?"

"We haven't talked about it yet," I admit. "But eventually, I'd like that." I risk a glance at Tessa, who is staring at the ground with a frown. "But for now, we'll stay at the house."

Axel gives a stiff nod. "Any thoughts on claiming?"

It's another thing I haven't discussed with Tessa, and I inwardly kick myself for coming here so unprepared. "It's early days."

"So, you want me to pull you from long distance runs while you trial and error this?" he asks, arching a brow.

"It's not like a normal relationship," I say, rubbing my thumb over the back of Tessa's hand. "We have to take this slow to make sure it's what Tessa wants." This gets her attention, and she gives me a quizzical glance. I turn back to Axel. "This could be because I took her, or because I was her first." Tessa slips her hand from mine and folds her arms over her chest, staring back down at the ground. "We need to make sure it's for real before we talk about claiming."

Axel gives a nod. "Okay, understood. Go do what you gotta do."

I grin. "Thanks, Pres."

"I'll take you off duty for a week. Come see me again, so we can see where you're at."

Tessa pushes to her feet and walks out. I stare after her confused, and Axel smirks. "Welcome to relationships, brother, where you have to learn to read minds and watch what you say at all times."

I find her just outside, and I smile to myself. "Didn't get too far?"

She glares at me. "Is that supposed to be funny?"

I shake my head. "Nope. What's up?"

"You're doubting me," she snaps. "I tell you I love you, and you're doubting that."

"I'm not," I say gently, stroking a hand through her hair and trying to get eye contact, which she actively avoids. "We just need to be sure this is for real, Tessa. We haven't spent any proper time together. We're going on feelings that developed at a time when you were distressed and scared. We have to get to know one another again." When she doesn't reply, I sigh. "Which is why I'd like us to take the dogs and stay back at the farm."

She finally looks at me. "What?"

"Let's go back to where it all began."

"You think going back to the place where you held me captive is a way to test or prove our love?"

I groan. "I'm not trying to get proof, Tessa. I know exactly how I feel about you. But let's stay in the middle of nowhere, where no one can interrupt us, and learn about each other all over again."

CHAPTER 21

TESSA

I'm not sure how to feel about going to the farm. Under different circumstances, it would be a place I'd love. The farmhouse is cute and homely, and I love that it's in the middle of nowhere, like a secret hideaway.

We load King and Gigi into the van and head to the house. Chance is sleeping on the kitchen floor, but he perks up the second he sees me. The other dogs rush to him, and he cowers while they sniff him. Eventually, he rolls onto his back, and this seems to please Gigi, who struts off like the queen she is. King sits beside Chance and licks his eyes. "Well, that went better than I expected," says Pit, holding up a can of dog food. "I hate giving him this crap, but it's all I had on hand," he says, opening the can and forking some out onto a plate. "At the farm, I got a whole freezer of meat cuts and chicks."

"Chicks?" I repeat.

He laughs. "What do you think they'd eat in the wild?"

"But they're not in the wild," I remind him.

"They need a good diet of raw meat, eggs, and vegetables."

I screw my nose up. "I think you can be in charge of his diet."

We load everything we need into the truck before setting off, making one stop at the pet store on the way to purchase everything Pit thinks Chance needs.

~

As the truck slows outside the farmhouse, my stomach lurches and my anxiety spikes. The good memories are very few, and my brain is assaulted with bad ones. I close my eyes tightly and breathe in through my nose and out through my mouth. "You good?" asks Pit, and I open my eyes to find him watching me with concern.

"I hated the way you used to look at me," I whisper.

He instantly looks guilty and reaches for my hand. "Who I am when I'm in club mode is not the real me. This is me," he says gently, offering a small smile. "When I have to do shit like that, I can't afford to be nice or show kindness. When I'm like that, I have one thing on my mind—protecting the club." I give a stiff nod. His explanation doesn't make the bad memories go away.

We get out the car, and he lifts Chance out, placing him on the floor. He takes a few wobbly steps as we both smile like proud parents, and for a second, I forget my anxiety.

Once inside, I lay Chance's bed beside the other two in the kitchen and then busy myself unpacking the food we'd brought with us. I didn't get to look around the kitchen before, and now, as I open cupboards to see the old China plates, I feel myself relaxing some more.

"They were my grandmother's," he says from behind me as he places our bags on the floor. "I daren't eat off them in case I break them. I'm too heavy handed."

"They're beautiful." I turn back to him. "Did you live with them here?"

He shakes his head. "No. I was a young lad, and I wanted to be where my friends were. There's nothing here for a teenager," he says, smirking, "but they'd insist I come over for holidays and they'd slip me money and feed me up. They hated her, my mother."

"Were they her parents?"

He shakes his head again. "No, my dad's, but he died when I was a baby serving in the Army. They reckon it's what sent Mum off the rails."

"That's so sad."

"I have no regrets," he says, shrugging.

"Did they keep photographs?" I ask hopefully, and he laughs.

"We'll walk the dogs and then I'll show you."

We walk around the field slowly. Chance is still struggling to stay upright, and we don't want to tire him too much. Halfway around, we stop, and Chance lies down gratefully. I sit beside him on the grass, and Pit joins us. "Have there been many?" I ask, feeling my cheeks burn with embarrassment.

Pit narrows his eyes. "Many what?"

"Girlfriends?"

He grins. "Is that what you are now?" he asks, his tone teasing. For a second, I'm transported back to school and the way Steven would tease me. As if he senses my panic, he grabs my hands in his. "This is real," he tells me firmly. "Don't doubt that."

"I'm just waiting," I whisper.

"For what?"

"For you to realise I'm this broken, ugly mess. And then you'll run a mile and laugh that I even thought for one second I was good enough to be with you."

His heart breaks for me, I see it written all over his face, and he gets up on his knees, facing me. He places his hands either side of me and crawls over my body until I'm lying back, staring up into his eyes as he hovers over me. "You're not ugly or broken, Tessa. You're fucking amazing. You've been through so much, and here you are, with me. After what I did, I don't deserve it. And so, it's me waiting for you to run a mile and tell me all the things I already know, which is that I'm not good enough for you."

I run my hands over his cheeks, pushing my fingers into his hair. He closes his eyes, and I pull him down to meet my lips. "I think maybe we're just perfect for each other."

He deepens the kiss, running his hand along my thigh, and then he suddenly stops and rolls from me, dropping onto his back and staring up at the sky, panting hard. He throws his arm over his face, and my eyes scan down his body to the bulge in his jeans. I bite my lower lip and take a deep breath before climbing over him. He uncovers his eyes. "Tessa," he whispers, sounding pained.

"Please," I murmur, rubbing myself against him. "We won't know if I'm ready unless we try."

He groans, half in frustration and half in pain. I smirk,

knowing I'm going to win as I push my hands under his shirt, enjoying the feel of his skin under my palms.

"I'm not gonna touch you unless you tell me to," he promises, placing his hands behind his head.

I grin wider. "You're giving me control?"

He gives a slight nod, his face suddenly serious. "It's what you need."

I push his shirt up and take in his toned abs. Leaning closer, I gently kiss his warm skin. I inch down his body as I trace kisses lower, gripping the button of his jeans and gently tugging it open. I glance up to see him watching me with caution.

Chance has gotten bored, and he wanders off to find the others, leaving us alone.

I lower his zipper, and he lifts his hips so I can drag his jeans down his thighs. I leave them at his knees and hook my fingers into his boxer shorts. His erection springs free, and I lick my lips as I take it in my hand and rub my thumb over the end, scooping up the bead of pre-cum and licking it. Pit's eyes darken, and I smile at him as I run my tongue over the tip of his cock. He hisses as I suck him into my mouth and cup his balls, just like he'd showed me to.

When he's groaning in pleasure, I let him fall from my mouth and crawl back up his body until I can feel his cock pressed against my underwear. "Can we try?" I whisper.

He nods. "Back pocket, wallet," he pants.

I reach into his pocket and pull out his wallet, opening it and arching a brow at the wedge of bank notes there. He smirks, and I pull out a condom. I rip it open, and he takes it from me, making quick work of rolling it over himself. I stand, shimmying out of my underwear, which he takes from me and places in the inside pocket of his kutte.

Hovering over him, I grip his cock in my hand and rub it against my opening. It feels nice, so I carefully lower onto him, moving slowly as he opens me up. I place both hands on his chest, closing my eyes as he fills me inch by inch. Once he's in as far as I can take him, I still, staring down at him. He's still got that cautious look about him, like he's waiting for me to break.

I begin to move, and he moans in pleasure. "Touch me," I whisper.

"Where?"

I take his offered hands and slide them under my shirt and to my breasts. He cups them, and I'm relieved I didn't put on a bra today as he teases my nipples. I move faster, needing to release. "Jesus," he mutters, squeezing his eyes closed.

I feel the warmth spreading up through me, causing my body to shake uncontrollably, and then it hits me, ripping through me. I shudder hard, dragging my nails down his chest. Pit grips my waist and thrusts up into me, chasing his own release. When he finally stills, his chest heaves and his breaths are rapid. I lie against his chest, smiling as his fingers run through my hair.

"Are you okay?" he eventually asks.

"Yes," I whisper, running my own fingers over his nipple. "Amazing. I told you I wasn't going to break."

"We still need to be careful, Te. Trauma comes out in all forms and at any time."

"I just need to feel normal again," I tell him. "And to put all that bad stuff behind me."

As promised, when we return to the farm, we snuggle up on the couch as Pit opens his grandma's photo album.

I study every image of his baby face, running my finger over his chubby cheeks. He was a cute baby and a cuter toddler, with dark hair and blue eyes, along with a killer smile. "Do you think you'll ever be a dad one day?" I ask. I feel him stiffen and glance up. "Pit?"

"No, Tessa. Kids aren't something I want." I nod, going back to turning the pages. "What about you?" he asks.

"Me either." I feel him staring and meet his eyes again. "What? It's okay for you to not want kids but not me?"

"Women usually want kids," he says, frowning.

"I'm not bringing a child into this world to go through all the shit I've been through. Humans are too cruel, and I don't have the heart to see my own kid suffer."

"Not every kid gets bullied or goes through what you have."

"What's your reasons?" I ask.

"The fear of retribution," he admits. "I've done too many bad things, and karma will eventually catch up. Whether that means I'll end up in prison or dead, I don't know, but I can't leave a kid to suffer alone."

"But you wouldn't. Your child would have a mother."

"Well, like I already said, you'll wake up and run a mile, so we won't even get to the kids stage." He slides his hand down the front of my top and cups my breast. "But we can keep practising."

PIT

I watch Tessa move around the kitchen wearing just my T-shirt. She finally places a plate of bacon on the table and is close enough for me to grab her. She giggles as I pull the shirt from her body, leaving her naked. I run kisses across her chest, taking her nipple into my mouth and swirling my tongue over the swollen bud. "Always naked," I whisper against her skin.

"What happens when we have to go back to reality?" she asks, swatting me away and picking up a piece of bacon. She leans against the worktop, watching me as I pile up my plate with pancakes. "I'll have to be fully clothed at the clubhouse."

We've spent the last couple days wrapped in a bubble consisting of just the two of us and the dogs. We've avoided talking about going back to the club and what happens tomorrow when I've arranged to meet Axel to discuss my future, mainly because I can't stand to see the look of sadness in her eyes when I mention the MC.

"You will," I agree.

"Unless . . ."

"We can't stay here," I say firmly, guessing it's what she wants. "The club is part of me, Tessa. I can't walk away." Just the thought of it makes me sick to my stomach.

"What if I don't want to be a part of it?" she asks tentatively.

It's the sentence I've been dreading. "That's what this week was about, right?" I ask casually, trying to sound unaffected by her words. "To see if we could move forward together."

"I want to move forward with you," she rushes to say.

"And with me comes the club." I slide the plate of food away, suddenly losing my appetite.

"It's just, living there . . ." She trails off. "It's a lot."

"They're my family, Te." I stand, closing the gap between us and taking her hand. "And they'll be your family too."

"What if I don't want a family? What if I'm happy with just you?"

I smile sadly, cupping her cheek. "We're kind of a package deal, Te."

"Would you seriously split up if I chose not to be a part of the damn club?" she demands, shoving my hand from her.

I take a few steps back. I've yet to see her really angry or upset, and we're yet to have our first disagreement. "You haven't even given them a chance. You might love the club."

"I doubt it. We're already arguing and we're not even back there yet."

"You've forgiven me, right?" I ask. She folds her arms over her chest but gives a nod. "So, you can forgive them too."

"Maybe if you weren't part of the club, you wouldn't do such awful things," she snaps.

"You're upset," I tell her. "It's understandable after everything. Take a walk and then we can talk."

She scoffs. "I don't want a walk."

"You don't want to fight either, Tessa. Not with me."

"Because you might lock me up?" she yells.

And there it is, the blow she's been holding back. We stare at one another for a few silent moments, and then I leave the room, whistling for the dogs, who come running, following me out the door and into the field.

I haven't been alone since we arrived, and I realise I don't miss it like I thought I would. Having her slip her hand in mine as we stroll together makes me happy. Happier than I've been in forever. But the club gives me security and stability. I don't know who I am without them. Or I do, and he wasn't good either.

I sit in the middle of the field, occasionally throwing a tennis ball and watching all three dogs run after it. Chance has begun to put on weight, and he's running just as well as the other two now. This break has done him good.

I hear soft footsteps behind me, and then she's standing before me, still naked but looking a lot less angry. I lean back on my hands and look up at her. "I'm sorry," she whispers. "I didn't mean that."

"You did," I say, "and it's okay. You have every right to get upset." I nod to my lap, and she lowers onto me, wrapping her legs around me and her arms around my neck.

"I'm scared," she admits, pressing her nose into the crook of my neck.

"Of what?"

"Being with all those people."

"Tessa, they're my family. Just as good as any mum or dad, brother or sister. It's like I get to live with my siblings and cousins all in one big house."

"Exactly. *Your* family, Pit, not mine. You've had sex with some of them."

I smirk. "They meant nothing."

"They'll hate me."

"You'll be an old lady, and they can't ever disrespect you."

"An old lady?" she repeats.

"If we're doing this, we're doing it right. You'll be my old lady. Property of Pit." I like the sound of the words as I say them out loud and find myself smiling. "And you'll share my family. They'll protect you like they would me."

"It sounds too good to be true," she mutters.

"Please, just give it a chance, Tessa. I promise you won't regret it." I reach between us, opening my jeans and pulling my cock free. It's been at least an hour since I was inside her, and now I've asked her to be my old lady, I need to feel her again. She doesn't need words as I pull her to me, pushing at her entrance until I slide inside her. We both release a satisfied sigh, and suddenly, things feel good again.

CHAPTER 22

TESSA

The dogs don't seem phased by our return to the clubhouse. However, my heart is heavy as we enter and head for Axel's office. Lexi is sitting on his desk, and he's got his head rested against her stomach as she strokes her fingers through his hair. He looks tired and maybe even vulnerable.

When he senses us approach, he releases her, and she stands, smiling at me. I return it, still feeling sick with nerves.

"The lovers return," says Axel dryly. "Are we celebrating?"

"Yes, Pres," Pit confirms, and Axel grins. It's the first real smile I've seen from him, and I relax slightly. At least he looks happy.

He stands, rounding the desk and holding out a hand for Pit, which he grasps, and they shake. Axel tugs him closer and gives him a quick hug, patting him on the back. "Congratulations, brother." Then he turns to me, and I shrink back slightly. He notices and holds out his hand. I slip mine into it, and he gently brings it to his mouth, placing a kiss on the back. "Welcome to The Chaos Demons, Tessa." I feel a warm buzz and smile in return.

"This calls for celebrations, right?" asks Lexi.

"I'll call the guys," Axel confirms.

"Actually," says Pit, glancing at me, "Tessa isn't into all that fuss."

I squeeze his hand, shaking my head. "It's fine. I'll be fine."

"Are you sure?" he asks, his eyes full of concern, and I give a nod. It's tradition for the club to celebrate, he told me that already, and I don't want things to be different for Pit.

Lexi claps her hands together in excitement then grabs my hand. "Let's go and make plans."

Pit keeps hold of me, refusing to let her drag me away. He gently strokes a hand over my cheek and pulls me closer. "You okay with that?" he asks. I nod, feeling my heart swell with love that he checked. He releases me and shoots a glare at Lexi. "You keep the club whores away from her. She ain't ready for their shit."

"Pit," she hisses, narrowing her eyes, "we don't refer to them as whores anymore."

"I ain't interested in your women's rights speech, Lexi. Keep them away from her."

Lexi salutes him, giggling as she leads me into the main room, which is quiet. We sit on a couch, and she sends off a text. "I'll gather the troops," she tells me.

"Sorry about Pit," I mutter to fill the silence. "Ebony didn't really like me and—"

She rolls her eyes. "Ebony doesn't like anyone. She's

been waiting for someone to sweep her off her feet, and she gets disappointed each time it doesn't work out. But now Pit's claiming you, she can't be a cow, so relax."

A few women rush in from upstairs. "Where's the fire?" asks one.

"Sit," orders Lexi, and they each fill a space on the other couches.

"Pit has claimed Tessa," she announces, and the women screech with excitement, each getting up to hug me and wish me congratulations. "And now, we need to plan a party."

The door opens and Anita saunters in looking amazing as always. "Did someone say party?" she asks, lowering her sunglasses. I rush to her, and we hug. "I've missed you this week," she tells me. "The office is a mess, and I hope you're ready for the pile of filing I've left on your desk."

I grin as we sit down. "I missed you too."

"So, Pit's finally come to his senses?" she asks, and I nod. "I hope he doesn't think you're not working cos I ain't giving you up for no biker," she warns.

"So, let me introduce you properly to everyone," says Lexi. "I'm Lexi, obvs, and I'm Axel's old lady. Duchess is unattached, although I think my dad would argue differently," she says, winking at Duchess. "She's been running the guys for years."

"Since I was classed as too old to be a whore," says Duchess, laughing, and we all join her.

"Coop is my dad, and he's got a soft spot for her. They hang out all the time and tell me they're just friends, but I know that look on his face and it ain't screaming 'just friends'," Lexi continues. "We also have the wonderful Luna."

"Also ex-whore," says Luna, giving a little wave.

"She's Grizz's old lady. He's the Vice President," explains Lexi. "Gemma is with Fletch. We're both ex-cops. And you know Anita already. Again, she's not strictly attached to any of the men, but we all kind of know she's Atlas's old lady."

"I really am not," says Anita, her tone bored.

"Only because you're stubborn," points out Duchess.

"Technically, when the shit goes down, we're only supposed to watch out for the other old ladies, but times have changed, and I make sure to include everyone I feel is a part of this club, club girls and all," Lexi says. "We're all here to look out for the men. We all want the same thing."

"Great speech," says Gemma. "Now, can we talk colour schemes and alcohol?"

I relax immediately. Pit was right—they're being really nice, and I don't get any bitch vibes off any of them. Maybe being here, having a new family, won't be so bad after all.

∼

Pit is watching me. He's spent the last half-hour sitting patiently at the bar, just watching me. Lexi leans closer. "I think your man is getting annoyed with me keeping you here. We can sort the rest. Go spend some time with him."

I smile gratefully. "Okay. Thanks."

"I'll call you if there're any problems." All the women

took turns putting their number in my phone, and then they added me to their WhatsApp group.

I slide my arms around Pit's neck, stepping between his open legs with our eyes burning into each other's. He makes no move to touch me as I press my body against his. "I like them," I whisper. "I now have six contacts in my phone." I remember Mark and smile. "It would have been seven, only I lost one." He arches a brow, and I place a kiss along his jaw. "Mark," I whisper.

He stiffens slightly. "Say his name again." He's daring me, and I smirk.

"You deleted his number," I accuse, laughing.

"And blocked it."

"Did you delete my pictures?"

"Yes. And from now on, any man who touches you will leave with broken bones."

"Harsh," I say, nipping along his jaw.

"Axel's given us a new room," he says.

"Didn't you have a room before?" I ask.

"Yeah, but it was on the whores' floor," he says, smirking. "We now have a respectable room, and you'll be closer to the other old ladies."

"Umm, upgraded," I tease.

"Shall I show you?"

I slip my hand into his. "Yes, please."

PIT

"Do you ever regret it?" I ask Axel as he places a tray of shots on the table. Grizz and Fletch dive in, each grabbing a glass and knocking the liquid back.

"No," he says firmly. "Never."

"You're not getting cold feet already, are you?" asks Grizz, slapping me on the back before picking up a shot and handing it to me.

I knock it back, wincing as it burns my throat. "No. I find myself waiting for her to realise this isn't what she wants. I can't relax."

"That's because you've not made it official," offers Grizz. "I felt the same. That's why we married."

"I'm not sure she'll go for that," I say, laughing.

I watch Tessa with the women, laughing and joking like she's always been a part of this club. She looks relaxed and at ease, something I never thought would be possible after what she's been through.

The last few days have been amazing. She's really come out of her shell, and I have Lexi and Anita to thank for that. They've made sure she felt welcome and a part of their circle.

Chance nuzzles into her side, and she runs her fingers through his silky hair. I've woken every single day with that fucker snoring between us, but he doesn't leave her side, like he knows just what she needs. Maybe he's a blessing in disguise because he's certainly helped her to relax around the club. She even moves around the place with ease. Every time a brother approaches her, he's standing to attention, ensuring no one gets too close.

"She ain't gonna vanish," Fletch says, waving a hand in front of my face to get my attention.

"He doesn't stop watching her," Grizz points out. He's right—I'm always watching her, checking she's okay. The need to be near her is intense, but she doesn't seem to mind. In fact, she tells me she finds it reassuring, which only feeds my obsession more.

"Yah know, Lucas can marry you here," Axel suggests. "Just say the word."

My heart twists. I'd marry her right now if she agreed, but I don't want to rush her. I shake my head. "She's not ready."

"Have you asked her?"

"No, of course not. The second I mention marriage, she'll run for the hills."

"I think she'd surprise you," says Fletch. "You said she's had some bad trauma, she needs security more than anyone."

"You think?" I ask.

"I know," he says with a nod, "she'll want to feel safe. Talk to her about it."

"Anyway, she's still married," I remind them.

"I can easily sort that," says Fletch. "I'll log into the records and delete it."

I smirk. "Just like that?

"Yep."

∼

I TAKE TESSA'S HAND, and she slowly spins, showing off the short dress she allowed me to choose for her to wear to dinner. I've never had a dinner date before, and I wouldn't feel comfortable taking her to a posh restaurant, and neither would she, so I arranged for the women to transform the club's kitchen.

I lead Tessa into the room, and she gasps, taking in the

twinkling lights strung up around the place. The table is set for two with a flickering candle in the centre. "I didn't think you'd want to go out for dinner," I say, pulling out her chair.

She slides into it. "This is perfect."

I take a seat to her left and lift the lids from the Chinese takeaway. It's Tessa's favourite. I spoon some rice onto each of our plates, followed by a little something from each container. She loves variety, and we often order several things from the menu to try.

"Are you looking forward to our party on Saturday?" I ask, pouring her a glass of wine.

"After the crazy week I've had at work, yes," she says, scooping up some of her rice. "I'm looking forward to it." I'm surprised by her confession, and she laughs. "I'm not that much of a recluse."

"If I'd have said to you a few weeks back that you'd be partying at the clubhouse, you'd have never believed me," I say, smiling.

"No, I guess not. But these last few days here have shown me that, actually, everyone can be nice, even Axel."

"We just take care of our own," I say, tucking in to my own food.

"I like that," she says, nodding. "And I like that they've made room for me too."

I place my fork down, suddenly feeling nervous. "I know we've not really talked about it, but what do you think about marriage?"

She stops mid-chew, staring at me. "Why?"

"I know you don't want kids, but you never said anything about marriage."

"Erm, I guess I never thought anyone would ask me the question," she admits with a nervous laugh.

I slide from my chair and land on one knee. She watches me through wide eyes as I produce a ring box from my pocket. "I'm asking," I say, opening the box to reveal a square pink diamond ring. "Tessa Dean, will you marry me?"

"Holy shit," she whispers, staring at the twinkling ring. "Yes, of course, I will."

Relief floods me as she throws her arms around me, falling to her knees. I laugh as she kisses me, and when I pull back, her eyes are shining with happy tears. I take the ring from the box and gently slide it onto her finger. "I'm glad you said yes cos I have Lucas booked for Saturday."

She gasps. "This Saturday?"

I panic. "If you want to wait, we can. I just thought you wouldn't want the fuss and organising something big and fancy wouldn't be your thing. Unless it is, in which case I can hand over my bank card and you can go crazy—"

She cuts me off with another kiss. "Stop talking, Pit," she whispers against my lips. "You know me better than anyone, and this is exactly what I want."

"Really?"

"Yes."

TESSA

The good thing about growing up mainly alone is that I appreciate the little things no one else seems to notice. Like the way Lexi touches me gently on the arm whenever she passes. Or how Gemma throws her arm around my shoulders when we're all together and chatting about life. It's things they do to one another all the time, they probably aren't even aware they do it. But I notice, and it means something to me. It means I'm accepted and I'm liked, the two things I've wanted for so long, and they give them so freely.

And they all understood my reluctance to walk down an aisle alone. The thought of a roomful of bikers, all watching me walk towards my future, was too scary. So now, as I stand at the doorway to the pretty, white marquee which had originally been hired to house our claiming celebration and has now been turned into a ceremony room, I feel at peace. The things that haunted me for so long are all gone.

Lexi hooks an arm in mine, Luna does the same on the other side, and behind me, Gemma holds a small bouquet of posies she handpicked from her own garden of flowers. It matches the bouquet she made me.

Music begins to play, and I take a deep breath as everyone inside stands. "Ready?" asks Lexi.

I give a nod, and we enter the marquee and make our way towards the front, where I see Pit waiting patiently. The second his eyes land on me, he relaxes. I see how his shoulders drop a little and a smile spreads over his face. He insisted I kept the dress a surprise, even though we've done nothing traditionally. I only chose it last night after Lexi organised for me to have a small hen party in the dress shop. She knew the owner, who was only too happy to host us. We'd spent hours all trying on dresses while drinking Champagne and wine. It was magical.

Before I've reached Pit, he's moving towards me, and I

laugh. He slides his hands along my jaw, his eyes tracing over every inch of my face. "You are beautiful," he whispers, kissing me gently.

Lucas clears his throat, and a few of the bikers laugh. Pit slides a hand into mine, and I realise the girls have all sat down in the front row. He leads me to the front, where Lucas is waiting to marry us.

PIT

The ceremony was short and sweet, exactly what we both wanted. If I could have whisked Tessa away to an abandoned island in the middle of the sea, I would have, because everyone being here wasn't important to me. Marrying her was all that mattered.

I march over to where she's laughing with the girls and take her by the hand, gently leading her away. "Rude," Lexi singsongs after us.

"You've hogged my wife for long enough," I call back.

I pull Tessa into my arms and bury my nose in the crook of her neck while running my hands over her backside. "I asked for five minutes," says Tessa, laughing as her arms circle my neck. "The girls have worked hard on this wedding, and I should spend some time with them too."

"I gave you ten minutes, and I hate not being near you."

She laughs again, placing a kiss on my cheek. "How do you cope when I'm at work all day?"

"He calls me constantly to check you're okay," Anita pipes up from where she's sitting at a nearby table.

"Oh my god, Pit, tell me you don't," she whispers.

"Just keeping you safe," I murmur in her ear. "Can we slip away?"

"No. It's our wedding day."

"But we've done all the big stuff. Now, I want you to myself. Besides, you hate people, remember?"

She runs her fingers through my hair, and I close my eyes, loving the feel of her every touch. "I thought you asked Tatts to brand me," she reminds me.

I'd almost forgotten. "Fine. Then can we slip away?"

She shakes her head in amusement. "We'll see."

∼

Seeing my name on her skin is the icing on the cake. It's her first tattoo, and I savour the feel of having another of her firsts. She watches intently as Tatts runs the ink over my chest, filling the gap over my heart with Tessa's name in large letters.

"I was watching you with Luna's kid earlier," I say, hooking my little finger around hers.

"She's a cutie," Tessa says with a smile.

"Maybe we were being too harsh when we said we didn't want kids."

Her smile fades a little. "Huh?"

"I'm not saying right now, but maybe we shouldn't rule it out completely. I think having a mini you to obsess over might feel alright."

A small smile pulls at her lips. "Yah know, somehow, you make everything sound possible."

"Think about it. The kid will have a lot of family. Big, strong bikers who will smash shit up if she hurts."

"What if it's a boy?"

"Then he'll be just like his dad and his uncles." I tug her closer. "I know you worry they'll be bullied or hurt in some way, but I swear that won't happen. I'll kill anyone who even tries."

"You'll be a brilliant dad," she whispers.

"With you to help me," I add.

Her smile spreads across her face, and she places a kiss on my lips. "Anything is possible when we're together."

And she's right. Fate brought us together in the most unusual circumstances, and although I regret the way it all began, I don't think we'd be at this point without being forced together. I'll spend my life protecting Tessa so she'll never have to feel scared or upset again. She's my world, and I'm hers.

"I love you," I tell her. "Now, can we slip away?"

THE END

ACKNOWLEDGMENTS

As always, thanks to my readers who support me and read everything I write. And also my team, who work their schedules around me because I am incapable of sticking to one. x

SOCIAL MEDIA

I love to hear from my readers and if you'd like to get in touch, you can find me here . . .
My Facebook Page
My Facebook Readers Group
Bookbub
Instagram
Goodreads
Amazon
I'm also on Tiktok